/19

DATA HUNTER

Robert Moonsinger, internet private investigator, receives visitors from three US government departments. They want him to find out how funds from banks — including the Federal Reserve — and important schematics of a secret military prototype have been stolen, and by whom. A lucrative offer is made, and he agrees to take the case — thus endangering his own life and that of others close to him. For Moonsinger is pitched against a vast criminal organization, headed by an utterly ruthless man for whom murder is the weapon of choice . . .

STEVEN FOX

DATA
HUNTER

Complete and Unabridged

1800043949

LINFORD
Leicester

First published in Great Britain

First Linford Edition
published 2018

Copyright © 2018 by Steven Fox

A catalogue record for this book is available
from the British Library.

ISBN 978–1–4448–3947–0

Published by
F. A. Thorpe (Publishing)
Anstey, Leicestershire

Set by Words & Graphics Ltd.
Anstey, Leicestershire
Printed and bound in Great Britain by
T. J. International Ltd., Padstow, Cornwall

This book is printed on acid-free paper

1

The owner of Moonsinger Internet Investigations was busy at his desk. As he looked up from his computer screen and through the picture window, he saw two men and a woman crossing the street toward his office.

He stood up and walked to the coffee machine, checking to see if he had enough freshly made to be hospitable to these potential new clients.

Robert Moonsinger was a middle-aged man of average height with high cheekbones; a straight, generous nose; weathered, copper-tinted skin the shade of an old one-cent piece; and straight black hair that was stiffened by the closely barbered cut that he preferred. His intelligent eyes were those of a skilled hunter and tracker.

Robert had just finished setting up his coffee maker for a new pot when the three people stepped into his office's outer room. The tall, statuesque black woman was the first to speak.

'Mr. Moonsinger?' she asked as she and her companions showed him their badges and ID wallets. 'I'm Matisha Waterman from the Department of Justice, and these are my associates: Juan Aguirre from Homeland Security, and Rick Sorenz from the Secret Service.'

Both men were at least six feet tall and appeared to be in good physical shape. The gentleman from Homeland Security sported a full but well-trimmed mustache, and a small scar along the bottom of his chin. The Secret Service man was clean-shaven and without obvious scars. As they entered Robert's office, the men removed their jackets. Rick's left arm had a long scar from an old wound just below his elbow.

After everyone had received coffee and sat down, Robert asked, 'What can I do for the government today? I don't believe that I've done anything that would warrant the attention of *three* departments.'

'It's not so much what you've done as what you could do for us, Mr. Moonsinger,' Matisha answered. 'You have a reputation for being able to track down various internet criminals, and to present law enforcement with the needed evidence for the DA to get a conviction.'

'I have helped in one or two problems in the past,' he conceded. 'Most of the time, I just help uncover scams before my clients can get too badly hurt, and maybe help them recover some of their losses.'

'Of course,' Juan said, 'you would expect some form of payment?'

'The normal fees of my profession, naturally,' Robert replied. 'Internet usage and office rent have to be paid somehow. The police pay me a straight consultation fee. Citizen clients pay the usual one hundred and seventy-five dollars per diem, plus normal expenses. Of course, since most of my investigations are conducted online, my expenses are minimal.'

'And what do you consider minimal, Mr. Moonsinger?' Rick wondered. 'What kind of expenses do you charge for?'

'I charge ten dollars an hour after the first six full hours of internet usage, and the cost of damages, if any, done to my computer in bringing a case to a close.'

'What kind of damages has your computer received in the past?' Waterman asked.

'Usually it's things involving specialized virus removal and such,' Robert told her. 'One time, though, someone threw acid on my machine. I had to replace all of my equipment. Fortunately, I'd just placed the backups of all my files, records, and programs in my safe.'

'How are you at tracing a hacker to his or her source computer and physical address?' was Aguirre's question.

'If you've been checking me out,' Robert replied, 'then you know that I'm one of the very best. Why don't you just state what you need from me, give me the facts, and stop with the questions? None of us has the time for BS.'

'Mr. Moonsinger — ' Agent Waterman smiled at him. ' — a large amount of funds and highly sensitive documents have been stolen from federally secured accounts. Supposedly unbreakable pass-words were breached. The thieves have apparently left no complete internet trail.

I understand that you use your instincts from tracking physical-world criminals in your internet hunts.'

'Knowing how the hunted think and react, and the efforts that they might use to hide their trail, will often lead to the revelation of the minutest of clues,' the PI replied. 'As a boy, my family depended largely upon our skills as hunter-gatherers to obtain the bulk of our sustenance. I find it a useful mindset.'

Reaching into her briefcase, Agent Waterman pulled out a folder labeled 'Special Information'. 'In this folder,' she said as she placed it in front of her on the desk, 'is a summary of everything we know, or surmise, about the thefts.'

'We have had the best government specialists working on this.' Sorenz's voice held the hint of a sneer. 'It's doubtful to me that you could do better.'

'Is their thinking that of the prey avoiding the hunter,' Robert said softly, 'or even that of the hunter looking for its prey? Putting oneself in the mindset of either, or both, is essential in finding skilled hackers who wish to hide their intrusions. The inability to think like one or the other can blind one to any clues available.'

Sorenz glared at Robert Moonsinger, apparently unwilling to drop his adversarial attitude. 'That sounds like you're bragging, Redskin' he jeered.

'No brag,' Robert replied coldly and calmly, 'but fact. Do you have a problem with me, Paleface? Because if you do, you can finish your coffee and leave; this consultation is over. Insults won't find your perps!'

'So,' Rick laughed, 'you *are* human and not just a walking, talking machine.' He glanced at his colleagues. 'I think that if he's willing to take the contract, we have our hunter.'

'Controlled enough to get the job done,' Aguirre agreed, 'yet passionate enough to want to see the job through, in spite of any obstacles.'

'I apologize for my colleagues,' Matisha added. 'We've interviewed several of your peers, but they all failed our little tests in one form or another.'

'A black woman, a Latino, and a

northern European.' Robert looked his guests over. 'At least one of you should know better than to throw epithets around, especially to one whose culture and land you've stolen. However, I'll accept your apologies at least . . . until you've made your pitch. I *am*, after all, still a free agent.'

'As I said,' Agent Waterman continued, 'the facts of the cases are in this folder. Briefly, about three months ago, one of the largest national banks noticed an anomaly in its accounts. Federal auditors were called in, and they discovered a larger discrepancy than the bank's auditors had found. The losses were traced to several online banking accounts that had all been opened, and then closed, within a month of each other. When a Federal Reserve bank where several national banks held their excess deposits began to notice unauthorized transactions, the Treasury Department and Secret Service were contacted.'

'When our investigations dead-ended with several overseas transfers, we suspected that groups hostile to the US were possibly involved,' Agent Sorenz picked up the story. 'Homeland Security has a longer reach than we do, so they were asked to help. Since all of the security and legal departments are under the umbrella of the DOJ and the NSA, the investigative lead was assigned to them.'

'We've interviewed several investigation agencies and single private investigators,' Agent Aguirre added. 'Your name came up as one of the top five people with the computer and internet skills — and a reputation for confidentiality and integrity — that we needed.'

'That's all very flattering,' Robert remarked, 'but what exactly is it that you wish me to accomplish?'

'Find the trail after it disappeared,' Agent Waterman told him. 'To our experts, the trail's grown cold and petered out. If you can find it and follow it to the thieves' den, your government would be very grateful.'

'How grateful?' Robert always became skeptical when government types spoke of gratitude. Usually they wanted things done for as little as they could get by with, if not free.

'The ten percent recovery fee that has been offered by the banks would add up to the low six figures,' Agent Sorenz replied. 'However, since schematics for a highly confidential military prototype have also been compromised, the government has added enough to bump the fee into the mid-six-figure range. If you accept, we are authorized to offer you a contract for that amount with a retainer of five figures.'

'That's very generous of you,' Robert agreed. 'However, *if* I take your case, we'll play the game by my rules.'

'And what are those rules, Mr. Moonsinger?' Agent Aguirre inquired.

'First,' Robert answered, 'I and my agency are not to be mentioned by name in any government report or any other communiqués of any kind. Second, I get paid in cash, non-traceable bonds, and/or T-bills. Third, I will only make weekly reports unless I have something that needs your immediate attention. And fourth, you come a-runnin' if I get into trouble. I won't appreciate being left twisting in the wind.'

The three representatives of their respective agencies looked at each other and seemed to come to a silent agreement. 'I'm sure that our superiors,' Agent Waterman spoke for the group, 'will agree to your first three conditions. As to the fourth, I can only say the three of us pledge to do our best to extricate you from any trouble you may find yourself in.'

'That means,' Agent Sorenz said as Juan Aguirre nodded in agreement, 'that I for one will go against orders if necessary. I *refuse* to leave anyone behind.'

'Then as soon as I receive my retainer,' Moonsinger told them, 'I'll begin my official investigations.' He came from behind his desk and shook hands with each of the agents as he said, 'We have a contract, sirs and madam. I hope, for the country's sake, that our uncle in the capital doesn't default.'

2

As soon as the government agents left, Robert began to peruse the folder that Agent Waterman had left behind. The report began with the accounting records made by the bank and federal auditors. Then he read the detailed reports of the money trace, which led to several European and two African international banks. From there, the money disappeared, presumably into banks in Switzerland and the Cayman Islands.

That seems to be where the crooks always want to hide their illegal funds, he thought. *Even the ones able to think outside the box are attracted to the confidentiality offered.*

When he saw the classified military prototype documents that had been compromised, he was surprised at the sophistication of the intrusions. The theft had seemingly left no evidence behind. The stolen plans were assumed to have been copied perfectly and then nearly all evidence of the intrusion removed from the dataset. The theft was eventually discovered when it became necessary to compare past results with the new data being received. Since the files on the prototype had last been accessed within four to six weeks before, the investigators had a timeline that fit perfectly with the bank thefts.

Accurate and precise timing, Robert jotted down in his newly opened casebook. *The suspects may have either had inside information or very good computer hacking skills. The final transference of the stolen funds may also indicate an unknown money laundering capability. This may be the reason that the funds became untraceable after going through so many foreign banks.*

* * *

The receipt of a thick packet from a government-insured courier company came two days later, containing his contract, his retainer, and the authorization codes to access the government files he would need to do his research properly.

'At least they've been faithful so far,' he commented to the seemingly lazy mongrel that had adopted him. 'Let's see if I can follow the trail further than the feds did.'

Opening up the files listed in the two reports given to him, and interfacing with his own specially designed activity tracing program, Robert used the passwords and authorizations he had just received. He had been working for an hour and a half when his computer began showing messages warning him of dangerous incoming files.

Immediate shutdown activated to protect data. Purge of files and programs initiated.

The words streamed across the screen as Robert pulled the power cord from its outlet and disconnected his computer from all incoming data sources. Using his cell phone, he dialed the direct line number to Agent Aguirre that he had been given.

'Agent Aguirre,' he said as soon as the line was answered, 'we've got a nasty intrusion countermeasure program buried in the files for the money trail and the prototype plans theft. I'll need to purge and reinitialize my computer, and hope that no permanent damage was done, before I can continue my investigation. If your computer experts had gotten as far as I did, several systems could have been compromised and shut down.'

'Has your computer been totally compromised?' Juan inquired. 'Will you be able to recover your data? Are you going to need to replace any of your equipment?'

'I won't know for sure until the purge is complete and I reboot the system.' Robert began relating everything he remembered from before his computer went into shutdown mode. 'It takes something really vicious for my computer to go into such a complete shutdown,' he said as he ended the conversation.

His computer software was designed to automatically remove dangerous files such as viruses, worms, Trojan horses, and logic bombs once the purge mode had been initiated. Removing the power source did not stop the purge. Removing the incoming data connections would keep new harmful data from intruding and complicating it.

After giving the program time to complete its work, Robert returned power to his equipment and typed the reinitialize command when the 'C' prompt was available. 'Okay, Mr. Dog,' he told his canine companion, 'let's see how much damage was done, and if any of our recent work was saved.'

The computer hummed to itself for several heartbeats, and then the screen displayed:

Drive reconstituted and reinitialized.

After finding and calling up the files that had been automatically saved up to the purge and shutdown, Robert began backtracking his work to locate the trigger for the IC attack. He was happy to find that the purge and reinitializing process had been able to save almost all of his work as well as his programs and files.

Before he reconnected with the internet, he began working on a program to get past the countermeasures he had run into. If he succeeded in designing an efficient response to the intrusion countermeasure program, a government patent would provide a nice steady income for when his caseload was slow to nonexistent.

'Well, Mr. Dog,' he said when he finished writing the code, 'if this works, neither of us will ever be forced to go hungry again.'

3

'According to Mr. Moonsinger,' Agent Aguirre told the others at their specially called meeting, 'our systems may well have dodged a very large bullet. While following the trail that he had uncovered, his machine suffered a serious attack. He quickly shut down everything he was doing and then ran a purge program. After that was done, he reinitialized and found that he'd lost very little of the data trail he had been following. The trail had been leading to a series of bank accounts that had not been known for clandestine practices in the past.'

'Has Mr. Moonsinger been able to bypass the difficulties he encountered?' Agent Waterman questioned.

'Robert informed me that he believes he's written a program that should prevent any new attacks,' she was told. 'He was having another go at the data trail as soon as he double-checked the data's backtrail for any unwanted codes that may have survived his purge.'

'It sounds as if our data hunter is more than just a highly skilled hacker. Who would have guessed from his background?'

* * *

Robert Moonsinger's internet backtrail had appeared clean. He went forward past the IC attack for about forty-five minutes when a sophisticated firewall program stopped his progress. He reflected that it looked as if he was stopped until his battering-ram program could break through the firewall's protection.

Robert got up to stretch his legs. Mr. Dog raised his head and wagged his tail in anticipation.

'Okay, Mr. Dog.' Robert laughed. 'I guess it's time for you to get some exercise.'

When Robert pulled the leash down from its hook, the dog made a happy bark and gave up all pretense of laziness.

'If you behave,' he was told, 'I'll add some meat scraps to your Gravy Train tonight.'

With the leash attached to the dog's collar, they left the office, the door locked securely and automatically behind them.

During the walk to the dog park, Robert considered the level of protection he had run into while tracking these internet criminals down. This was too high-tech for ordinary everyday computer gangsters. What were they planning that needed to be hidden so thoroughly? It had got to be worth a lot of money, something that could be real nasty, or both.

Mr. Dog came running up to him after only a few minutes of visiting with the other dogs and their owners. Seeing something attached to the dog's collar, he found what appeared to be a note.

'Whatcha got there, fella?'

The note was on a piece of plain white printer paper. When Robert unfolded it, he found a typed warning to stay away from the feds and to back away from his investigation.

Robert quickly reattached the dog's leash and headed back to his office. When he got home, he found the place surrounded by several emergency vehicles, the street bathed in red and blue flashing lights. The door to his office had been knocked off of its hinges, and the big picture window was cracked and smoky.

'That's my office, Detective,' he told the plainclothes officer standing off to the side. 'What happened here while I was away from the office with my dog?'

'The owner of the pharmacy across the street reported seeing masked vandals breaking into the place after she heard a loud crash,' the detective told Robert. 'After the perpetrators had gotten in, they apparently took a baseball bat or other blunt instrument to the computer and set fire to a lot of loose paper. When the uniforms arrived, they observed smoke coming from inside and notified the fire department, which was already responding to the building's alarm. The uniforms used extinguishers when a quick check of the scene while waiting revealed a lot of smoke, but no flames were visible. They entered and proceeded to smother the smoking debris. The fire crew is inside now checking for any hot spots.'

The detective and the PI asked and answered questions back and forth until the office was declared safe.

Mr. Dog's whine reminded Robert of the note that had been attached to the dog's collar.

'I don't know if this has anything to with the fire and vandalism, Detective,' he called out as she started to walk away, 'but it seems to fit in with a government case I contracted a couple of days ago.'

The detective turned back toward Robert and asked, 'Why didn't you say something earlier?'

'The agents were from the DOJ, HSD, and the Secret Service,' he answered. 'Also, when I returned and saw what had happened, I had other things on my mind.'

'Okay,' she said. 'Call them and have them get in touch with me.' She handed him a card with her contact number that read 'Shelly Brown, Detective III, Sandfield Police Department, Sandfield, CA.'

⋆　⋆　⋆

The emergency crews had left, the detective had cleared the place as safe for entry, and Robert was allowed inside to inspect the damage to his office and equipment.

'Well, Mr. Dog,' he said as he patted the canine's head, 'if you can stand the smell of smoke, the living quarters should be okay to stay in until we can have the place revamped. I think a better security system and a stronger door are needed, don't you?'

Mr. Dog sniffed at the debris and charred flooring, and then sneezed as he yipped his agreement.

'Let's get to work, then.'

An hour later, the debris had been placed in the trash bin and the smoke stains were only memories. Lysol and deodorizer had removed most of the stink from the air. Now it just needed the building inspector to declare the building structurally sound, and he could get estimates on repairs, Robert thought as he inspected his handiwork. Aloud, he said: 'I always knew that this place wouldn't burn that easily. Come on, Mr. Dog. It looks as if we're eating out tonight.'

The old-fashioned diner a block south of his office was busy but not crowded. The sidewalk contained special service areas with rings to attach dog leashes and racks to park bicycles. There were food and water dish holders built into the special area's concrete slab to serve the specialized menus for the customers' pets.

'The usual for Mr. Dog, Bob?' Sally inquired as he walked in.

'Add some shortbreads, too, Sal,' he told her as he sat at the counter. 'He's had a very disturbing day. His home's been violated, and I need to make sure he still feels wanted if he decides to put up with the hostile shenanigans of his human's enemies.'

'I heard about what happened,' she commented. 'Almost everyone who's come in this evening has had something to say about it. Theories, questions, rumors, opinions, and the like.'

Robert placed his order and waited for her to put the ticket on the cook's wheel. One of the busboys took the order for his pet out to where the dog was patiently waiting.

'Whatcha hear, Sal?' He spoke with a drawl that let Sally know he was intensely interested in the scuttlebutt being said about his recent misfortune.

'It came mostly from Jackie and the pharmacy's customers,' Sally replied. 'They said that there was a loud crash, and when they looked outside, they saw three men wearing ski masks going into your place. Jackie called the cops right away. By the time they arrived, the vandals had smashed most of your equipment and tried to set fire to your things. Of course, the fire department was automatically alerted when the smoke detectors went off. The three men ran out and headed south to Orchard Street, then east, away from the emergency crews.

'Jackie said these guys were in and out before she finished her report. Did they bypass your alarm system? Breaking down your door should have brought the cops before Jackie's call was made. No one seems to know how they were able to have the time to smash up everything and set the fire.'

'That'll be one of the things I'll be looking for when I get a copy of the police and fire reports. Anything else being said?' Robert asked.

'Some people,' Sally answered, 'are wondering about who those people were who came to see you the other day.'

'What kind of wondering are they doing?' His face was a mask of stone. 'Anything specific?'

'Just things like 'Who were those strangers?', 'Did they case your place during their stay so that they could set you up and steal something from you?', and 'Why would three well-dressed and official-looking people pay such a quick visit?''

Sally continued to do her best to fill Robert in on the local gossip being generated as he ate. He was only slightly surprised at how fast the flow of rumor was being disseminated. As he finished his meal, he decided that for now, it was probably in his best interests not to interfere. Disinformation was often helpful in the early stages of any investigation. The police report would give him his best outside source for factual information.

'Come on, Mr. Dog,' he said as he untied his canine friend. 'Let's see if the place has aired out enough so that we can sleep there tonight.'

Mr. Dog wagged his tail and put his paws on Robert's chest.

'Yeah.' He rubbed the dog's ears affectionately. 'I love you too. Time to go home.'

When he got back, Robert's cell phone began to play the 'William Tell Overture.' There was no caller ID and he didn't recognize the number, but he answered it anyway.

'Mr. Robert Moonsinger?' the caller said when he answered the call. 'This is Ms. Waterman's assistant at the DOJ. She asked me to check with you and make sure that there were no problems with the information packet we sent you.'

'Nothing was wrong with the information,' he told the agent's assistant. Then he spoke before he had thought things through. 'However, the people you have me investigating are not only very good at covering their backtrail, but have laid some very vicious electronic ambushes to protect themselves from discovery. Agent Aguirre has my report. Also, our unknown subjects have knowledge that they shouldn't about their adversaries.'

'Are you in any physical danger?' the DOJ assistant exclaimed.

'Nothing that I haven't handled before.' Realizing that he may have said too much to someone he did not know and was not sure of, he disconnected abruptly. Unless he was absolutely positive who it was he was talking to, he should not divulge anything more than he felt he had to.

He saved the number of the caller and dialed Rick Sorenz, the Secret Service agent. Agent Sorenz answered on the third ring.

'Agent Sorenz,' Robert said, recognizing the agent's voice immediately, 'does Agent Waterman have an assistant who makes calls to check on non-government contractors?'

'Not when the contractor has stipulated a routine for reporting as you have,' Sorenz was quick to reply. 'Did someone call you?'

'I just got off the phone with someone at this number.' Moonsinger read off the phone number he had saved. 'The ID wasn't blocked, but it was only the number of the originating caller.' He reported all of the events of the day, and the rumors that Sally had told him that were floating through the town's gossip chain. He also gave him Detective Brown's number and said that she had asked to be called.

'Officially,' Agent Sorenz told him, 'we can't be very informative, but maybe we can trade some information. I'll also check out that number you just gave me. Maybe we'll get lucky.'

Robert and Sorenz went over in detail the events of the past few days since their meeting.

'I'll write up a report to give Agents Waterman and Aguirre,' Rick said as they were ending the conversation. 'If you have people you trust to do the repairs and get the new equipment you need, go ahead. When you've the completed bill, send us copies and we'll reimburse you. Also, when they're done, we'll send out a company to upgrade your security system to government standards. Agent Aguirre or I will be on site to supervise and clear the people doing the installation. Do you still have a copy of the program you wrote to get by the intrusion countermeasures you ran into?'

'My SOP is to make copies of any new programs that I write or acquire and place one in my safe,' Robert told the agent, 'and another in my safe-deposit box when it is one this important. Since I haven't had time to get to the bank, both copies are in my safe. The vandals didn't have time to crack it. First thing when the bank opens tomorrow, into the safe-deposit box both copies go.'

'Sounds good. See you in a few days.'

4

Early the next afternoon, the building inspector arrived and soon pronounced the building as sound. Since Robert had transferred all of the items in his safe to his bank's safe-deposit box that morning, he called the company he always used for repairs and renovations. He was told that the owner would arrive that evening to estimate the work to be done.

When the contractor arrived, Robert showed him the inspector's report.

'He didn't think that it'd be a major job to fix everything back to code,' Robert told him as they walked through the building.

'Good thing you own the building outright, Bob,' the contractor said as they reviewed the repairs that would be needed. 'If you had a landlord, he'd probably be looking for a way to break your lease. This is, what, the third time in two years your place has been broken into?'

'The fourth, actually, Ralph,' was the reply. 'You wouldn't think that people who use the internet to commit their foul deeds would be so vicious, would you?'

'I just use the internet to do some advertising,' Ralph related to Robert as he shrugged his shoulders. 'And even then, I have a company I've known and trusted for years design everything on the website. I always send my final bills by snail-mail. My email is where most of my business inquiries come from. Otherwise, I make out all of my business forms and do my accounting records offline.'

'For most people,' Robert commented, 'they're safer that way.'

When Ralph and Robert had finished their walk-through, Ralph handed him an itemized estimate of the cost of the recommended work to be done. Then he told him, 'Things are slow right now, so we'll be able to begin work tomorrow. After we remove the damaged drywall, flooring, and such, we'll order the materials and wait for them to be delivered. You should allow about ten days for the prep work, and for the materials to arrive, and then maybe another week or two to get it all finished. Say about a month in all to get everything back into top shape.'

'Send me the final bill,' Robert replied. 'My contractor will reimburse me. Now I just need to shop for a new computer system.'

'I've heard a lot of good things about the new laptops,' Ralph claimed. 'All the computing power of a desktop, and they're totally portable.'

'Yes, and they make a good grandfather or great-grandfather backup system. They also make a great way to have the files that you need immediately on hand when you're in the field.'

*   *   *

Robert had driven to the computer store where he always purchased his supplies and upgrades.

'Good morning, sir,' the salesperson

greeted him at the door. 'How may I help you today?'

'I need a complete replacement for my old desktop system and its peripheries,' he told her as her eyes lit up with the prospect of a major sale. 'I'd also like to look at your top-of-the-line laptops. Anything I buy will need to be completely compatible with my new system.'

'You're doing a complete upgrade?'

'Yeah, I was sorta forced into it.'

The salesperson showed him the most expensive models until Robert was able to make her understand exactly what he required.

'Ah,' she finally said. 'I think this model has what you're looking for. Lots of storage space on its internal hard drive, and the external hard drive has an extensive backup potential. The inkjet color printer has super-large individual cartridges for the black and each of the regular and day-glo primary colors for perfect color reproductions. The flatbed scanner and fax machine are the best quality available. The quality versus price ratio is among the best in the industry, and it includes a two-year warranty.'

'Seeing as how this is a replacement for malicious mischief,' Robert responded, 'I may not use the warranty, but I'll take this unit anyway. Now I'd like to look at the laptops. I'll need the same requirements as the desktop, but in a portable form that'll hook into the desktop's peripheries.'

A short time later, the salesperson rang up his order and asked, 'Where shall I have this delivered?'

Robert gave his address and then asked, 'Can the delivery be delayed until next month? My office is being renovated and I have no place for installation until the work is done.'

The store manager was conferred with, and he readily agreed to hold delivery for a customer making such a major purchase.

'We'll need to ask for half now, and the balance at the time of delivery,' the manager said. 'Will you need any assistance with the installation?'

'No, thank you,' Robert replied. 'I can do everything myself once it arrives.'

Robert paid half of the purchase price and made arrangements for the delivery in a month. Pocketing the receipt, he walked out to the parking lot. On the way to his car, he noticed a van with dark windows a few spaces from where he was parked. Having just had his place broken into and his computer attacked from an online program in an attempt to wipe out his hard drive, he took special note of the vehicle.

'Not this time,' he said to himself as he made a call to Detective Shelly Brown.

'Detective Brown.' Her direct line was answered quickly.

'Detective Brown, this is Robert Moonsinger. I maybe acting paranoid, but after what happened to my office the other day, I'd rather be paranoid and safe rather than sorry.'

'I remember your situation, Mr. Moonsinger,' Brown said in a professional tone of voice. 'What has you concerned?'

'I've just been shopping for a replacement computer at the Tenth Street Electronics store,' he told the detective. 'When I came out, I observed a red Ford minivan parked one aisle behind my car and two spaces to the right. All of the windows are tinted too dark to see inside, and the license plates are missing.'

'You're right to be concerned after what happened, and they have enough violations for a routine traffic stop. I'll have dispatch send a cruiser over to check it out. Are you going to be leaving the parking lot right away?'

'I thought it best to appear as natural as possible so as not to arouse their suspicions.'

'Okay. Take the most direct route back to your office. If they appear to be following you, call me and I'll redirect the uniforms.'

'Will do, Detective Brown.'

As Robert started his car and pulled out of the parking lot, the van started up and left in the same direction. As he passed a large shopping center with several open parking spaces, he saw a police car coming from the cross street that he had just passed. The cruiser fell in behind the minivan. After a block, the police pulled the van over to the curb.

Robert was about to breathe a sigh of relief when several loud pops and the sound of screeching tires caused him to check his mirrors. Spotting an open entryway into the shopping center, he quickly found himself a space and speed-dialed the emergency number. When he was connected, he gave his name and location, followed by a quick and detailed report of what had occurred.

'I have no knowledge of the officers' conditions,' he told the operator. 'I heard what may have been shots and screeching tires. I looked in my mirrors just in time to see a red minivan pull away from the scene and the flashing police lights, which haven't moved.'

'I have the police and paramedics headed to the location,' the dispatcher informed him. 'Please stay near the scene so your statement can be taken.'

Within a short space of time, but one which seemed like forever to Robert, he observed sirens and flashing lights approaching the area of the stopped police vehicle. Carefully, he got out of his car and walked to the curb. He waited for someone to approach him before he said anything or moved closer.

'Are you the person who called this in to 911?' the officer asked when he got within easy speaking distance.

Robert admitted that it was indeed he who had reported the incident. He also explained the events of the past few days which had led up to his phone conversation with Detective Shelly Brown, and why the officers had stopped the minivan.

'What happened after I talked to Detective Brown has me feeling partially responsible,' he said sadly. 'Are they going to be okay?'

'Fortunately,' the officer reported, 'their Kevlar vests absorbed most of the force from the bullets, and they just have deep bruises. They'll probably be back on full duty after a couple of days on medical leave.'

After answering several more questions, and relating a detailed description of the minivan and giving the last direction he had seen it heading, Robert was released after he had promised to sign a written statement at the station the next day.

Somebody, he realized, didn't want him on this case. There must be something that he was not aware of right now. Perhaps he should take delivery of the laptop and start downloading everything concerned with this case . . .

When Robert finally returned home, he let Mr. Dog out into the fenced-in backyard of his office-residence. While his canine friend romped and chased birds, Robert prepared the dog's evening meal. When everything was ready, Mr. Dog was called into the house to eat, rest, and spend the rest of the evening sleeping.

No matter how Robert evaluated the last week, the only reason for the physical and electronic attacks aimed at him had to be related to the case he had just received.

'I've really stepped into a quagmire,' he murmured as he sat in his chair and stroked Mr. Dog. 'I don't like working while being made to wear blinders.'

Robert relaxed in his chair and soon fell asleep. He awoke at dawn, still in the chair, stiff and sore. Mr. Dog had let himself out through his special door during the night and had not returned inside.

Deciding to check on his canine friend, he went to the back door and called quietly. When he got no answer, he began to check for the dog's whereabouts. The dog had stayed because Robert had given him food affection, and had seen to his health. It had never been forced to stay, but it was unusual for him to leave the fenced area of the property without Robert and a leash.

In a dark corner, Robert found the animal tied up like a calf at a rodeo. Carefully, he undid the ropes and other restraints, all the while repeating soothing sounds. After Mr. Dog was free, Robert gently checked him for wounds and possible broken bones.

'As soon as the vet opens in the morning,' he told the dog, 'I'm taking you for a complete check-up. This time they've gone too far! They can come after me, and it's to be expected; but when they attack my best friend and companion, they're meat for the grinder.'

He helped the dog back into the house.

Robert had decided to wait until the alpha shift at the station began to make a report on the attack of his pet. Meanwhile, he would wait for better light before checking his backyard for signs of his unwanted visitors. He also decided to see if his place had been invaded during the night.

He couldn't believe that someone could have done what they had to Mr. Dog without him being awakened by the dog's struggles and barking. The animal had to have been tranquilized somehow, and only beginning to rouse when Robert awoke. It was a good thing that he'd awoken when he did, or Mr. Dog might have injured himself from having his jaws tied shut and trying to get free. Robert continued to comfort the animal, and to make sure that he hadn't been hurt in some way that he was not aware of.

'I know that you did your best, Mr. Dog,' he said, 'to protect the both of us. Sometimes humans can be so cruel.' As a reward, and by way of comforting him, Robert gave Mr. Dog one of his special treats.

When the sun was fully up, Robert went out to his backyard and took a good look around. Near the back fence line he spotted a large piece of uneaten raw meat. He placed a marker beside the meat as Mr. Dog sniffed at the bait and growled low in his throat.

So, Robert thought as he observed the dog's reaction, Mr. Dog hadn't trusted their offering. Good instincts and a wise decision. He'd ask the police to check the meat for poison or a tranquilizer, then try and find out how they finally *had* overpowered the dog without waking half the neighborhood.

After he had reported the late-night visitation, Robert meticulously checked the ground for footprints and signs of a struggle between the intruders and the dog, placing markers at the spots that he knew to be recent disturbances in the lawn.

By the time Detective Brown and her partner arrived, Mr. Dog was doing much better, and was ready to be introduced to the detectives and to accept them into his small circle of close friends.

'I'm going to take Mr. Dog to the vet for a check-up and blood work,' he told the detectives. 'He seemed suspicious of the offered meat, but he still appears to have been drugged. They must have done *something* to him before he was tied up.'

After telling Detective Brown that he was expecting a contractor to start repairs, plus explaining about the markers and that the gate would lock itself when they left, Robert drove Mr. Dog to the small animal hospital in the downtown area.

After hearing what had happened to the dog during the night, Dr. Ward, the veterinarian, checked his patient for any sign of abuse, and then drew a small amount of blood.

'He shows no signs of overt abuse, and *if* he was drugged, Mr. Dog now appears to have fully recovered,' Dr. Ward informed Robert. 'However, we may not find any residual traces of a sedative in the blood sample.' He smiled. 'Okay, Mr. Dog, you've got a clean bill of health. If those culprits bother you again, make sure you get them to leave some DNA or

43

other evidence for the police to follow up on, okay?'

Mr. Dog gave a bark of agreement and licked the doctor's face.

'You're a good dog, fella.' Dr. Ward laughed as he ruffled the dog's neck fur.

★　★　★

The contractors arrived before Detective Brown was done. She called Robert and, after a brief conversation, was told that Ralph and his crew were indeed the contractors, and to let them into the office so that they could begin work.

'I'm on my way home right now,' Robert informed her.

As he drove, Robert attempted to fit things that had been happening during recent days into a logical pattern. He was sure that the attacks on his computer were related to the job from the government, but what were they looking for in his papers?

He always copied his notes and daily journal onto a DVD and placed it in his safe before leaving his office. Any work that had to be left on his equipment was encrypted with that day's code, making him feel as safe as possible from hackers or break-ins into his office. Printouts were shredded as fast as he read and copied them electronically.

As he pulled into the parking area of his home and office, he was greeted by an officer in uniform. 'State your business and show me some ID please, sir,' the policeman ordered non-combatively but firmly, 'and make your movements slow and easy.'

'I'm Robert Moonsinger, the owner of Moonsinger Internet Investigations, Officer.' Robert carefully removed his PI license and his driver's license. 'I've just returned from taking my dog to the vet for a checkup. Detective Shelly Brown will vouch for me and Mr. Dog. Or the contractor will. Ralph is doing some renovations for me.'

After carefully looking over Robert's identification, the officer handed it back. 'Do you always have this much security, Mr. Moonsinger?' he queried.

'No, but I think I probably will from

now on, if the government has its say.'

'The government?'

'Three agencies have asked me to do some work for them.'

Robert parked his car in his attached garage and went inside to his living quarters. As he passed through, he looked in on the work being done in his office.

'Hey, Bob,' Ralph greeted him. 'So far things are looking good. Physically, the office looks to be in great shape except for the smoke and water damage. I think we'll know for sure what needs to be replaced by midweek. We may be able to finish in only two, two and a half weeks.'

'That sounds great Ralph,' Robert returned. 'Mr. Dog will be glad to have everything back in place. And the new smells will interest him for a while. I've arranged for my new computer equip-ment to be delivered in a month. If you're done early, perhaps they can bring it out.'

'You can have your desk and all of the file cabinets refinished while we get the walls done and repainted. All of the odors should dissipate by the time your new stuff arrives. We can install a steel security door if you'd like.'

Moonsinger thought a few moments. Then he told Ralph, 'The client has offered to install government security upgrades. Perhaps we should leave that up to them. Why not place a heavy solid wooden door for now? At least then you can reuse the door.'

'Why not ask them about the door?' Ralph asked. 'It'll save you time and money to have their input right away.'

'I'll call them in the morning and arrange a time for them to get with you.'

5

In another office not far away, two men were explaining themselves to a third.

'Why did you open fire on the police?' the man with Eurasian features sitting behind the metal utility desk asked the two men in front of him, while giving them a cold, unforgiving stare. 'Now the cops will never give up until the two of you are in their hands!'

Pushing a button on his desk, he called two hard-faced men into the office. They stood at attention, awaiting orders.

'Take these two incompetents away,' he told them. 'After they have learned what becomes from not being able to stay out of trouble, place them where they can redeem themselves for their actions.'

Before the two seated miscreants could react, the hard faced men each made quick movements and the sound of popping necks was heard in the room. 'We'll place them in their van and make sure that it's found,' the bigger of the two men said as he and his partner placed the now-deceased over their shoulders and carried them to the hidden garage.

Pressing the button on his intercom, the man at the desk said, 'Send in the housebreakers.'

★   ★   ★

The housebreakers left the office in a subdued frame of mind.

'What does he mean by calling us stupid, lazy dolts?' the short, dark man in the lead complained. 'All he ever does is to sit on his butt giving orders!'

'You ever wonder why he won't come out from behind his desk, Rico?' the lean man in the middle asked.

'Why?' the Polynesian with well-toned muscles bringing up the rear wondered. 'He's just lazy, right?'

'No,' the second speaker replied. 'When he took over the business, several dudes disputed his right to leadership. They got together and attacked him in his home. When the dust settled, the malcontents were all dead, but he had been left a cripple in a wheelchair.'

'Bet a few bodyguards were iced for that failure.' Rico laughed.

'There weren't any bodyguards, dummy,' Rico was told. 'They'd all gotten a shiv in their backs for their loyalty. The Boss was left alone. He took out all of those guys by himself. I hear that the Boss took out the last two *after* his back was broken.'

'So we don't want him pissed at us?'

★   ★   ★

Detective Brown frowned as she talked to the pathologist and looked the scene over. The red minivan matched the description that the PI had given when he reported the possibility that he was being followed.

'The victims were killed somewhere else; and then they and the van were dumped here?' she asked.

'It appears that way, Detective,' the pathologist agreed. Then he elaborated, 'There's no sign of a struggle inside the van. Their necks were broken by somebody — or somebodies — very strong and professional. I'd guess that the victims were put into the van, driven to the dumpsite, and were arranged in their current positions before rigor mortis set in.'

'Time of death?'

'Sometime within the last twenty-four hours.' The pathologist rubbed his chin. 'I'll be able to fix it better once I get them on the tables.'

'Okay.' Brown scribbled a reminder in her notebook. 'Email me photos from the pathology records. Then I'll see if the officers recognize them, try to get a match with their IDs, and check for rap sheets.'

Feeling that she might be getting out of her depth, she called Moonsinger's cell as she returned to her unmarked car. When he answered, she told him about finding the van and its cargo in the parking lot of a defunct strip mall at the eastern city limit line. She then made arrangements to meet at the local Starbucks for a Q&A and brainstorming session.

'Bring any and all theories,' she advised him, 'as well as the evidence and information that your clients are willing to share.'

'I'll talk to them,' Robert said, 'I'll let you know everything I can. You may wish to check with Dr. Ward and see what the lab reports had to say about what was used on Mr. Dog to incapacitate him. He might have them back by now. See you soon, Detective.'

An hour and a half, a visit to his safe-deposit box, and several phone calls later, Robert pulled into the Starbucks parking lot. Detective Brown waved to him from an outdoor table when she saw him walking toward the entrance.

Robert held up one finger and then pointed toward the door. *Be with you in a just a moment*, the gesture implied.

When he had made and received his order, Robert went and sat down with Shelly Brown. 'An agent from Homeland Security is willing to meet with you at the Federal Court Building commons center at eleven-thirty tomorrow morning,' he said. 'I've also been authorized to give you full disclosure on my investigation.'

'That's a bit unusual,' Brown acknowledged. 'This must be extremely important for Uncle Sam to be so forthcoming.'

'I'd expect that they'll want tit for tat.'

Moonsinger and Brown discussed the events of the last week, each asking questions and giving answers while their drinks became tepid.

'Sounds to me as if these government types are using you as a stalking horse, Moonsinger,' Brown said after they each had refreshed their orders.

'The things that have happened seem more in keeping with expendable live bait,' Robert agreed. 'Even Mr. Dog's life seems to be on the sacrificial table.'

'Then why don't you claim they've breached your contract and get out from under the gun?'

'I've pushed too far,' Robert answered, 'and gotten in too deep to be allowed to quit. With these two deaths, I think I've learned way too much to be dismissed as someone who's not dangerous to the bad guys. Their intrusion countermeasures and heavy-duty firewall have been successfully countered. They can't allow me to continue.'

'Do you have any type of safety net?'

'Just the one between my ears, Detective.' Robert grinned as he replied. 'And the instincts I was born with. Promises have been made in good faith, but even the best of intentions can be made to go awry.'

6

Ralph and his crew were half an hour away from quitting for the day when a nondescript gray sedan circled through the neighborhood. Recent events had made him overly suspicious, so he took special care to notice if the sedan reappeared, and took down the license plate number. Bob wouldn't appreciate having the work done twice, he told himself. And if he saw that car again, he would definitely have to let the cops know.

While Ralph and his people were putting away their tools, the sedan slowly drove by the office again. Ralph activated his cell phone and dialed the police non-emergency number. After explaining the reason for his call and giving his name, he asked that the information be relayed to Detective Brown.

'She's been the lead investigator on the vandalism and arson of Mr. Moonsinger's office,' he reminded the person on the phone. 'She asked that if I saw anything or anyone suspicious, to get a message to her.'

Ralph had already sent his crew home. He was certain that the police would be arriving soon. He knew that Robert had gone to meet with the detective and decided to give him a call.

Moonsinger felt his phone vibrate and heard the 'William Tell Overture' ringtone as he and Detective Brown were walking to their cars. 'Moonsinger Internet Investigations,' he answered.

'Bob, this is Ralph. Are you still with Detective Brown?'

'Yes,' he replied. 'What's up?'

'A grey sedan has made two suspicious drive-bys in less than an hour. Detective Brown has asked me to report anything odd. I think that this qualifies.'

Moonsinger handed his phone to the detective as he told her, 'Ralph has a report for you.'

As Brown listened, Ralph related his sightings and his uneasy feelings. 'They're brazen,' he said, 'I'll give them that. They just drove by again.'

'Stay out of sight,' the detective ordered. 'I'm sending patrol officers now. Moonsinger and I are on our way. Observe and report mode, Ralph. Keep safe.'

Shelly gave Robert back his phone and turned toward her own car. 'Back to your place,' she told him. 'Ralph needs support.'

As she drove to Robert's office, she called the dispatcher and asked for backup. She confirmed that she had received Ralph's message when the dispatcher asked her about it.

She and the patrol officers arrived within a minute of each other. They parked in the pharmacy parking lot across from the detective's office. Shelly got out and walked over to Robert's car as he pulled into his private parking space. The officers walked into the pharmacy and asked the owner-manager to keep the clientele away from the windows and doors.

When the grey sedan had not returned twenty minutes later, Detective Brown gave orders for intensified patrols of the entire block of businesses and residences. 'There's no way of telling who they were casing for sure,' she remarked. 'If they aren't after the PI, maybe this will provide a preventative measure.'

Later, when Robert was getting ready for bed, he let Mr. Dog out for his evening's inspection of the grounds. When the dog had returned, Robert fastened the doggie door.

'If you need to go out before morning,' he said, 'you wake me and I'll go out with you. You don't want to be roped and hogtied again, do you?'

The dog woofed, then went and lay down in his sleeping spot.

Robert smiled. It was his belief that dogs understood a lot more than most humans gave them credit for.

★   ★   ★

Robert was awakened just after dawn by Mr. Dog's insistent pawing and whining. When he got up, thinking the dog needed to go out, he was surprised to see the

58

animal head toward the entrance from the garage instead of the back door. Mr. Dog began whining and pawing at the door, occasionally looking back at his master.

'One moment, friend,' Robert muttered, as he retrieved his weapon from the hiding place where it stayed when not in use. 'Now, let's see who's out there.'

Cautiously opening the now-unlocked door, Robert looked around his garage as he silently worked his way to the light switch by the workbench. He knew from the light coming from under the partially raised door that someone had broken in. Turning on the garage's interior light, he saw tools and other items scattered across his workbench.

'Whoever you are,' he said in his most forceful and authoritative voice, 'you have five seconds to show your empty hands and announce your reasons for invading my garage.'

Quick movement from the rear of his car and a shadow that disappeared underneath the garage door were his only answers.

'Mr. Dog,' he ordered, '*fetch!*'

Mr. Dog shot out under the door after the invader. As Robert opened the garage fully, he heard growls and a frightened gasp of pain. Keeping his weapon pointed toward the ground and away from his body, he headed toward the sounds of a desperate struggle between man and beast. He quickly came upon a man struggling to escape from his dog, who was pulling at him as if he wanted to carry him away someplace.

'Mr. Dog,' Robert said sternly, '*hold!*' Then, to the intruder, 'Just stay still and my friend won't hurt you. Answer my questions, and you might only be charged with breaking and entering with intent to do malicious mischief.'

'All right, mister,' the cowed man sobbed. 'Just keep that beast away from me!'

Giving Mr. Dog the signal to guard the prisoner, Moonsinger put away his weapon and dug his cell phone out of his pocket. He was quickly connected to the robbery/homicide department, and left a message for Detective Brown. The suspect made a couple of attempts to get away, but was stopped when Mr. Dog got to his feet and voiced a low growl of warning.

'You may want to send a forensics team to fingerprint the garage,' Robert suggested before he disconnected. 'A lot of my tools appear to have been handled.'

'You're sure that you have the right person?' he was asked.

'The perpetrator attempted to outrun Mr. Dog when he slipped under the partially open garage door,' Moonsinger related to the duty officer. 'So even if I'm not sure, he is.'

'That's sounds good enough to hold the man for questioning. What's your twenty? I can have someone pick up your suspect, and you can meet Detective Brown at your place.'

Robert gave his location, and sat on the ground to wait.

★   ★   ★

'The perp must have been extremely quiet,' Robert was telling Brown, 'because it was my dog who awakened me, not anything the intruder did. Mr. Dog headed straight for the garage when I got up.'

Detective Brown took notes and asked questions about the sequence of events.

'This appears to be a good citizen's arrest,' Shelly replied, closing up her notebook. 'We'll see what he has to say for himself after we compare fingerprints.'

'I just cleaned the tools on the bench a couple of days ago,' Robert told her, 'and I haven't used or moved them since. The metal should hold some good impressions, and he wasn't wearing gloves that I saw.'

'We've got some good prints from the garage door, Detective,' the woman dusting for prints said. 'We'll need to get prints from Mr. Moonsinger so that we can eliminate them from all the others. Is there anyone else who may need to be eliminated?'

'Not that I recall,' Moonsinger responded.

'There are some pry marks around the latch-bar, Detective,' the other forensics person told them. 'And some scratches around the lock. I think that we have probable cause for a B and E.'

'Good work,' Detective Brown praised her team. 'When you're done here, write up your reports and place them on my desk.' Ruffling Mr. Dog's neck fur, she added, 'You did good work, too!'

7

There was no more excitement for the rest of the week. Ralph had all of the damaged walls removed and ready for replacement. The wiring was also checked for any damage. Several of the wires were outdated, and were replaced as a preventative measure.

'When you have some free time, Bob,' Ralph advised, 'I'll come over and check all of the wiring. I'll not only make sure that everything is up to code, but able to take on a heavier load as well.'

'Go ahead and do it all at once,' Robert replied. 'I'm going to go ahead and have the laptop delivered so that I can work on the case from the motel's WiFi. I've got all of my backups ready to install to the new equipment. Something tells me that I need to keep on top of things in the virtual world.'

★ ★ ★

Robert drove to the door of his rented room. 'It's a good thing that Sandfield is so pet-friendly,' he told Mr. Dog as he unlocked his door. 'We not only have eateries with menus for animals, but rooms in motels that are set up for their furry guests.'

Mr. Dog looked around the room, sniffed all of the corners, and then lay down in the doggy bed.

'Let me know if you need to go out during the night, fella.' Robert brushed his teeth and showered. Mr. Dog was fast asleep by the time he was done and had turned out the light.

Early in the morning, Robert completed his ablutions and took his dog for a walk before breakfast. When he was done and breakfast was over, he drove to the Tenth Street Electronics store to make arrangements to pick up his laptop.

'I find that I have need of the laptop now rather than later,' he explained to the manager after showing him the receipt for his equipment. 'My office won't be ready for the desktop and peripherals for another week or two.'

'That's fine, Mr. Moonsinger,' the manager told him. 'Sometimes things change. Come on back to the computer department and we'll get the laptop that you selected.'

Robert took delivery of his laptop and returned to his car. There appeared to be no one stalking him this day. Just as he sat behind the wheel, his phone demanded his attention.

'Moonsinger Internet Investigations,' he answered.

'This is Detective Brown's partner, Detective Smith, Mr. Moonsinger,' the voice on the other end of the connection replied. 'We met at your place after your dog had been attacked. We'd like to talk to you about our meeting with the Homeland Security agent. Can you meet us in Detective Brown's office in, say, thirty minutes?'

'I'll be there, Detective Smith.' Moonsinger disconnected and then dialed Shelly Brown's cell number.

When she answered, he asked, 'Did you wish to meet with me at your office in thirty minutes?'

'Yes,' she told him. 'Detective Smith and I need to discuss with you what Agent Aguirre told us. With all that's happened since your pet was attacked, we haven't had time to make the arrangements.'

'Okay.' He breathed a sigh of relief. 'I told Detective Smith I'd be there. Sorry if I sound paranoid.'

'That's understandable, Mr. Moonsinger. I would be as cautious as you are in your place.'

Robert started his car and headed toward the police station.

At length, he pulled into the police visitors' parking lot; and, rolling the windows down just enough for Mr. Dog's comfort and safety, locked the car. His pet would be an effective watchdog.

Detective Brown's office was on the second floor, so Robert elected to take the stairs. When he reached the office marked 'Brown and Smith, Detectives', he knocked on the open door's frame.

'Come in, Robert,' Shelly said as she looked up from her desk. 'Smith was with me at the meeting with Agent Aguirre, so we can speak openly.'

Brown and Smith informed Moonsinger of several things that he had not yet been told, mostly things that had only recently been discovered.

'Aguirre told us that while they didn't know the identity of the persons involved,' Smith concluded, 'they did know the agency they worked for. An internet equivalent of a spy ring for hire.'

'The group seems to be based somewhere in California,' Brown added, 'and right now, all of their activities seem to be revolving around you and your work for the government. Aguirre seemed to think that there's a leak in one of their offices.'

'I had a call from someone at Agent Waterman's office not long after my office was broken into,' Robert informed the detectives. 'Did Agent Aguirre mention that I had spoken with Agent Sorenz of the Secret Service?'

'Not directly,' Smith reported, 'but he did mention that the lead to the leak came from you.'

'So they're still playing their cards close to the vest.'

'I'd assume so.' Detective Brown frowned. 'I can't say I blame them. Having someone inside your own organization betraying you can make you very wary of nearly all of your contacts until you can nail the SOB.'

'What can we do until then?'

'Watch our step and tread lightly,' Smith remarked, 'hoping the culprit makes a mistake before we do.'

'I still have the phone number from the caller ID in my cell's memory. Maybe the phone records can give us some help.'

'If we get lucky.' Shelly sighed discontentedly.

'Think positive, Detective,' Robert replied. 'Think positive.'

After the meeting, he played back the conversation with Agent Waterman's 'assistant' in his mind. He remembered the sudden uneasiness he felt as he continued speaking with her. His years growing up and his work as a private investigator had honed his instincts for BS as well as his survival skills.

'Listen when your spirit talks,' his mother's brother had told him as he was growing up. 'You may not always understand right away, but it'll place your feet on the right trail.'

Moonsinger got in his car and drove to the motel. *If only I could hear clearly*, he thought. There was much he needed to know. Perhaps he could gain insight from his dreams.

Robert poured dry dog food into the bowl provided by the management and prepared for bed. As he slept, he dreamed of a spider sitting in a chair, half of its legs shriveled against its body, unusable. This spider controlled other spiders from the center of its web, and caught many flies. The boss spider in the dream had the type of face that people called 'Eurasian'.

Why is the face important? Moonsinger wondered as the dream began to fade. *And what do the shriveled legs mean?*

Sunlight filtering in behind the window curtains roused the PI awake. As he sat up and put his feet on the floor, his pet raised his head.

'Good morning,' Robert said in greeting. 'Did you sleep well?'

Mr. Dog got out of the doggy bed and went over to the door to wait.

'Be with you as soon as I shave and get changed,' Robert said as he ran water into the sink. 'Then we'll see about getting some breakfast before we begin looking for signs along the internet trails.'

Half an hour later, Robert was at his bank, in a private room inside the deposit-box section. Having charged his laptop overnight in the motel room, he was now ready to input the programs and files he needed to research the databases that his government passwords gave him access to. It took him two hours to load everything onto the machine.

'My dog is going to be getting antsy out in the car,' he told the bank officer as he replaced everything in his safe-deposit box and put it back in its locked space. 'He probably thinks that I went away and left him.'

'I looked outside a few times,' the bank security guard told him. 'I think he made a new friend or two while he was waiting.'

'Fickle dog,' Robert laughed. 'He'll make nice with almost anyone, but he knows where home is.'

Robert whistled and Mr. Dog's ears perked up. He ruffled Mr. Dog's fur and patted his sides.

'Let's go back to the motel.' He unlocked the car door and got in. Now that everything was loaded onto the laptop, he could take another look at those ICs and that firewall. He had never seen such formidable protection before.

The drive back to the motel was uneventful except for a near-miss when a farm truck ran a red light. Robert cursed the other driver as he slammed on his brakes. Mr. Dog had been asleep on the backseat and was thrown to the floor. The alert driver behind him was just able to avoid a rear-end collision. Robert quickly checked the traffic as he crossed the intersection and pulled over to the curb to check on his pet. He was relieved when the animal showed no signs of injury.

'Some innovative animal lover needs to design a safety harness for animals traveling in cars,' he mused to himself as he pulled back into the flow of traffic.

Later, in his room, Robert began his renewed research. His program to counter the IC program got him up to the firewall, where his battering ram program began working on getting him past the formidable protection that the wall provided.

'Now we'll see what these people still have up their sleeves,' he told his furry confidant.

8

The Boss wheeled his chair over to the computer station when his master programmer called him over. 'He's back?' he asked as he looked past the programmer to the screen.

'And his invasive measures seem stronger than ever,' came the answer. 'He seems to have been busy while his equipment was being replaced. The IP address confirms a new system is being used.'

'Can he locate our system?'

'He's smart. Given enough time, he *could* figure out the algorithm for randomizing our IP address. Nothing is 100% unbreakable.'

'It is if he's dead.' The Boss rolled back to his desk, picked up the phone's receiver, and dialed a number. When the phone at the other end of the connection was answered, he asked, 'Do you still have a fix on our playmate? Good. Initiate 'wipeout'.'

The Boss held down the disconnect button on the phone's cradle and then dialed another number. 'Fold up the tents and disappear,' he told the person who answered.

Looking at the programmer, he told him, 'Shore up the computer defenses and transfer everything to the secondary and tertiary sites. I want all traces of our activities on the main site wiped clean and sanitized.'

'No one will follow us,' the programmer acknowledged. 'I guarantee.'

'Your life will depend on it, *I* guarantee,' the Boss answered.

★   ★   ★

The aide at the DOJ office of Matisha Waterman was cleaning out her desk, shredding papers, and wiping everything off of her computer when her boss and the FBI agents walked in.

'Going someplace, Ms. Jackson?' Agent Waterman said from behind the federal law officers. 'You seemed mighty interested in the affairs of a particular Internet

PI. I'm sure that Agent Aguirre will be extremely interested in your recent extracurricular activities. Agent Sorenz and several of his agents are in Sandfield right now. Take her away.'

The lead agent stayed behind as the other agents took Ms. Jackson into custody.

'What now?' he inquired. 'This case could go international.'

'Let's see if the Secret Service and Robert Moonsinger can get us more information,' she replied. 'We've managed to catch a medium-sized fish. Maybe she'll be able to lead us to the big fish.'

* * *

Outside cabin 16 at the Sandfield Rest Motel, three men in clothing designed to blend in with their surroundings quietly approached the door.

'The subject is liable to be armed,' one of them whispered. 'Take him out and don't hesitate. The Boss doesn't like interference.'

Inside, Mr. Dog growled a warning almost imperceptibly low, causing his human companion to reach for his weapon.

'You're better than any electronic alarm system, my friend,' he murmured as he positioned himself behind the door. 'The best security system is one with an early-warning device.'

The door was kicked open and the three intruders burst into the room, automatic weapons set on rapid-fire. Mr. Dog leaped for one of the men and clamped his jaws down hard on his gun hand. The man screamed and dropped his weapon as the dog worried the arm. A second man turned to face the furry attacker just as Robert fired a .45 round into his shoulder.

'Not my dog, you don't!' Robert yelled as he turned to face the third man in time to see his head explode.

'Federal agents!' voices shouted from outside. 'Everyone lay down your weapons and get face down on the floor!'

'Mr. Dog,' Robert commanded, '*back off*! The good guys are here.'

The federal agents entered the room with their weapons in hand. They checked the dead man, and then the wounded. Satisfied that the situation was under control, they picked up the dropped weapons and had Robert cautiously get up on the bed.

'Just to be sure that we've read the situation correctly,' the gray-haired woman in the black pantsuit said, 'carefully show us your identification.'

'When I've done that,' Robert said as he reached for his ID wallet, 'and in spite of you and your partner's timely assistance, I want to check *your* bona fides. Surely you understand?'

The agent scrutinized the wallet carefully. She then plucked her credentials from her jacket and said as she showed them to Robert, 'Agent Shirley Reid, Secret Service, Treasury Detail. And this is my partner, Agent James Black. Agent Sorenz has reassigned us to the Protection Detail to watch your back after recent events.'

'I appreciate the help,' Robert replied with an ironic smile. 'My people aren't used to the US Cavalry coming to their rescue.'

James Black, a thirtyish-looking man of mixed ethnicity, replied, 'Maybe it's about time things changed, right?'

Robert grinned as he held out his hand to his rescuers.

' "The times, they are a-changin',' ' he quoted.

★ ★ ★

As the paramedics and the coroner's van left, Shelly Brown and her partner, Detective Smith, stayed behind to interview the witnesses.

'The government will reimburse the motel's owner for the physical damages,' Agent Reid told the detectives. 'We'd like to move Mr. Moonsinger to our safe house.'

'The owner is understandably upset, and refuses to give Mr. Moonsinger another room,' Agent Black added.

'Yeah,' Robert replied, 'having one of his cabins turned into a Swiss-cheesed crime scene does *not* make for a happy man.'

Brown and Smith closed their notebooks and stood up.

'We'll need to get all of your statements down in written and signed form within forty-eight hours,' Brown informed the three main participants. 'This is most likely related to a major ongoing investigation.'

Agent Black, giving the two city law enforcers a hard stare, commented, 'I'm afraid that the country's security trumps your investigation.'

'We've been informed of you having hired Mr. Moonsinger and what he's been asked to do, Agent Black,' Detective Brown replied. 'Agent Aguirre of Homeland Security brought Detective Smith and me up to date earlier this week. These attacks are the ongoing investigation I spoke of. We've been placed under the National Security Act, so we are not at liberty to divulge much of the things we know without direct orders from Agents Waterman, Aguirre, or Sorenz.'

'So,' Agent Reid said, 'everyone is on a 'need to know' basis?'

'Especially me!' Robert blurted out. 'I can't do what I've been hired to do if I'm not fully informed. These people are clever, well-protected from internet prying, and as deadly as they are relentless.'

'You've learned more in two weeks,' Agent Black told him, 'than our people have learned in the whole three months that we've been aware of the problem. You could probably brief *us* on several things.'

'Such as,' Robert replied, 'that the funds which were stolen went to several numbered Swiss accounts, were transferred to a like number of accounts in the Cayman Islands, then placed in small untraceable accounts in African countries, and then back to new accounts in the Cayman Islands. After that, I don't know yet. I've written an anti-intrusion countermeasures program that's apparently working, and I'm also using a firewall battering ram to brute force my way into their files. Our adversaries are getting worried. How they know about me is troublesome. I've done my best to cover my internet tracks, but they seem to have followed me home somehow. I've been using a brand-new laptop since this morning. Give that information to your professional hackers. See if they can help protect me while I work on completing my internet tracking. The less time I have to spend looking over my virtual shoulder, the sooner I can give you what you need to close this case.'

Reid and Black agreed to have Agent Sorenz confer with his opposite numbers in the DOJ and Homeland Security, and get back to Robert on a secure and encrypted line.

9

The man captured at Robert Moonsinger's home had been placed in a special cell after having been through a strip-and-cavity search for any suicide devices. The cell was at the far end of the special, and ultra-secure, detention center's minimum-inmate and maximum-security block. 'If supervillains were real,' the facility's motto proclaimed, 'we could contain them.' However, like most places designed to keep people from getting out, getting in was not much of a problem.

The guard assigned to the special prisoner had replaced the newest guard on the roll call. He had a specialized pin coated with an undetectable toxin. He was told that if he succeeded in silencing his target, but failed to escape, his family would be well rewarded.

Since he had been assigned the quietest four-hour shift, the assassin was confident of success. He was not told that he was never meant to leave. The pin that the man carried was designed to slay both killer and victim.

When the guard on the following shift came on duty, he found that both the guard and the prisoner had expired with no obvious signs of foul play.

'Mission successful,' was the report given to the Boss.

'Failure and/or capture,' he told the next group assigned to the Moonsinger problem, 'is unacceptable. Either will be punished with extreme prejudice.'

The three persons given the task of seeing that Robert Moonsinger would no longer be a problem walked out the door, knowing that they might never come back for new orders.

'We've been Ninja-trained,' they said among themselves. 'Our honor must remain untainted. We will not fail.'

★ ★ ★

The departmental heads all of the nation's most elite law and security organizations had just returned from a meeting with the President.

'We've got to give the POTUS something he can place the country's hopes on, or we'll have a run on the banks that'll make the Great Depression look like a scratch in the dirt,' Waterman told her companions. 'Economic terrorism seems to be the next level. What can we do?'

'Let's not forget the prototype weapon,' Aguirre added. 'One use could bring this nation to its knees. Combined with the lack of faith in our banking institutions, we might never recover.'

'Have we sealed all of the leaks?' asked Waterman.

'We, and the FBI, believe that with Ms. Jackson's arrest, we have,' Sorenz answered.

'Let's triple- and quadruple-check for leaks, and see if we can't give Moonsinger the internet protection he needs to safely do his job,' Waterman ordered. 'We can't have our best data tracker compromised.'

Sorenz's cellphone began to vibrate on his belt. 'I'm not in the mood for bad news,' he said as he answered his phone on speaker, 'after the chewing-out the POTUS just gave me.'

'So,' Shirley Reid replied, 'I'll give you the 'okay' report before the 'not so bad' news. First, three men failed to take the PI hacker out at his motel. Two were taken into custody, and the third went to the local morgue.'

The other agents observed the scowl on their colleague's face and waited to hear what the rest of the news would be.

'Where's Moonsinger right now?' Sorenz demanded.

'He's been taken to Safe House Beta Fourteen, sir,' Reid informed him. 'He and his four-legged bodyguard were uninjured, but the room took extensive damage.'

'Four-legged bodyguard?'

'He's called Mr. Dog. He's a very smart and protective mutt,' the answer came back. 'According to Detectives Brown and Smith, he's helped capture one other suspect.'

'Tell me about that,' Sorenz ordered.

Reid explained about the break-in at Moonsinger's garage, and how Mr. Dog had been treated during an earlier attempt at the house.

'Has the burglar been questioned?'

'Not by us,' Shirley responded. 'But we have a transcript of Brown and Smith's interview, and access to the video. I don't think it would have been possible to squeeze him for any more info. He was only hired help, and was only told enough to do what he had been contracted for. Besides, he and a guard were found dead in his cell.'

'Okay,' Sorenz said as he was ending the call, 'stick to Moonsinger like a tick on Mr. Dog, and see what else you can find out.'

★　★　★

'That PI must lead a charmed life,' the African man complained. 'How does he keep avoiding being taken out? He certainly has wormed his way past our defenses.'

'His demise has now become our foremost objective,' the Boss told him. 'He's getting too close to our secrets. He already knows too much about our financial dealings.'

'Our insider in the police department reports that the Secret Service agents have taken him to a secret safe house. He is working on finding out where that is.'

'Do we have access to our captured operatives?'

'They won't survive another night, sir,' he was informed. 'Hospital security is easier to subvert than prison security.'

The Boss dismissed his lackey with a nod, and tapped a few keys on his computer. 'Initiate 'Tsunami',' the message read. 'Leave no one and nothing undestroyed.'

Moonsinger's annihilation was all but assured. The Boss sighed in satisfaction as he wheeled himself to his private rooms connecting to his office.

As he entered his suite, he told his manservant, 'A cup of Darjeeling, Michael, and the papers.'

'The *L. A.* and *New York Times* are on the coffee table, and the *Wall Street Journal* is on the nightstand by the bed, sir. The tea will be ready shortly.'

Michael had been the Boss's best find in domestic help — valet, butler, and all-round 'gentleman's gentleman'. If only his underlings in the business were as efficient!

The Boss picked up the business section of the *New York Times* and began his nightly perusal of current business trends. Michael brought a pot of hot water and a tea ball filled with his special blend of Indian Darjeeling tea.

'Will there be anything else, sir?'

'Nothing for now, Michael. I'll be retiring at eleven-thirty. I'll require your assistance then.'

Michael returned to his meal in the kitchen, and opened the book of fiction he had checked out from the library.

10

'Whose turn is it to make the food run?' Agent Black asked, even though he knew the answer.

'Yours,' Agent Reid and Robert replied.

'How 'bout Chinese to go?' Black inquired. 'Anyone have a favorite combo?'

'Orange Chicken and Pineapple Chicken,' Robert placed his order. 'All chow mein, no rice, and a spring roll.'

'Same here,' Reid said. 'Don't forget to bring our furry hero his special meat dish.'

Agent Black took out his car keys and left on the food run.

Robert worked a kink out of his back and went to the kitchen to pour himself a cup of coffee. The pot was fairly low; thinking that the others might like a fresh cup with their supper, he prepared to start a new one brewing while they waited for Agent Black to return.

The hospital corridors were dark and quiet. The two men dressed in the white smocks of orderlies pushed a cart toward the shared room of two recently admitted patients. The security guard stopped them at the door.

'Let me see your passes and authorizations,' he ordered them in a matter-of-fact, no-nonsense voice. 'These men are under Code One restrictions.'

The first orderly pulled out a lanyard with his ID from underneath his smock and held it up to the guard as he said, 'Time for their medications.'

As the guard inspected the pass, the second orderly took out a hidden short metal club and hit him behind the ear, knocking him into unconsciousness.

The two men placed the guard onto the bottom shelf of the cart. While one of the orderlies slipped into the hospital room, the other adjusted the cover on the cart so as to hide the guard. The first orderly took a hypodermic needle out of his pocket, uncapped it, and shot the contents into the IV lines of the sleeping patients.

'It's done,' he told his partner as he came back into the hallway. 'Let's leave Sleeping Beauty somewhere out of sight, and get out of here.'

Pushing the cart into an alcove, the two men removed their smocks and took the service stairs out of the hospital, disappearing into the anonymous night of the city streets, satisfied that they had done their job well.

★   ★   ★

At eleven-fifteen, the Boss's bedside telephone rang.

'Tell me that the garbage has been taken out,' he said.

'The first pick-up has been made,' the caller told him. 'We're working on the second pick-up.'

'See that 'Tsunami' is fully implemented,' the Boss ordered, and hung up his phone.

Michael entered to help his employer prepare for bed.

'See that I'm not disturbed until nine o'clock, Michael,' he said as he was helped into bed. 'It'll be a busy day tomorrow. I shall need my rest.'

Michael left the room to set the security codes for the night. He then set his alarm for seven-thirty. He would have time to prepare the Boss's breakfast and bring in the morning editions of the local papers and the morning's *L.A. Times*.

Now he could finish his book of fiction before turning in for the night. Reading was his favorite escape from the dull, humdrum life that he lived. The lives of the characters in books were full of excitement, danger, and romance. He wished that he had the imagination to write such stories — but nothing in his life seemed to lend itself to what he longed for. His dreams would remain just that — dreams.

★　★　★

At two o'clock in the morning, Reid, Black, and Robert were awakened by the constant throaty growl issued by their four-footed companion. Robert and his dog were herded to the rear of the safe house by the Secret Service agents as they gathered up their weapons.

'Both of you stay here until we give the all-clear,' Shirley told her protectees. 'Call this number and get us some help.'

Having left all the lights off, the two agents donned their low-light goggles and waited in hiding. They heard the quiet scratching of lockpicks being used on the front door. No amateur, this — the heavy-duty security locks were opened in record time.

Quietly, the door was opened, and three heavily armed persons sneaked into the house. Slowly and methodically, they searched the living room and the kitchen.

The intruders also wore low-light goggles. The fact that the agents had used this house before and knew where every room, stick of furniture, and appliance was located was now the only advantage — besides the ability of Mr. Dog to attack silently and from unexpected positions — that they and their protectee had.

As the intruders spread out to search

the house for those whom they expected to be asleep, Shirley and James stayed still, hoping for a chance to subdue their opponents silently one at a time. While they waited, the intruders revealed that they had another advantage — quiet communication between each of their members.

'We need to overpower two of them at the same time,' James whispered. 'Then maybe we can surprise the third.'

Without warning, a painful scream was heard from the hallway. The sounds of the struggle between man and enraged dog brought the other intruders rushing into the hall, where they were attacked from behind.

Reid and Black used lead-filled clubs to overpower their targets quickly, and told Robert that he could call off his dog — everything was under control.

★　★　★

'Mr. Dog just had all of his shots updated,' Moonsinger told the paramedic taking care of the person that had been attacked by the animal. 'He was only defending himself and us, as he's been trained.'

'We'll need his veterinary records,' the EMT stated. 'People are too happy to find an excuse for a lawsuit nowadays. You may also want to back up any episodes of his temper.'

The paramedics took the injured person to the prison ward of the hospital as the other two suspects were taken away for questioning.

'Let's hope that this guy didn't give Mr. Dog some blood-borne disease,' James Black commented as Detective Shelly Brown and Detective Smith approached. 'You can't be too careful nowadays.'

After all of the greetings were made, and everyone involved in the fight was questioned. The government agents gave precise details of their actions and their locations during the brief altercation. Robert, having been hiding in the backroom, told what little he'd been able to hear and see.

'When Mr. Dog bolted from the room

as I unlocked the door to get some idea of where everyone was, I found out how many people had broken into the house. I was relieved when Agents Reid and Black turned on the lights and said the code words for the all-clear signal,' Robert reported.

'Was that when you called your dog off the person he had down?' Shelly inquired.

'It was,' Robert replied. 'Why have him waste his energy when Agents Reid and Black had the other two suspects out cold on the floor? When they were all handcuffed, Mr. Dog relaxed, but wouldn't take his eyes off of them.'

Reid and Black also made reports to their superiors. 'Guard those three yourselves,' they were told. 'You are to be the lead during all questioning. The suspects in this case have a habit of turning up dead. You'll have support teams arriving ASAP. Check their bona fides thoroughly when they arrive.'

'Will do, sir.'

* * *

The prisoner that had been captured by Mr. Dog was treated at the hospital and placed under guard until the next day. After his release by the doctor, the suspect was escorted to the same special holding cells as the other prisoners.

The cells were thick steel-reinforced concrete, without windows. The doors were all made of super-hardened steel. The only other opening was a special slot just large enough to allow the food trays to pass through.

The special government guards were placed on six overlapping eight-hour shifts, with one pair of guards being rotated out every four hours. Therefore, four guards would be on duty at all times.

'The ventilation shafts are too small even for a young child to crawl through,' the person in charge was telling Reid and Black, 'and they're placed nine feet above the level of the bed and commode.'

'I still want the monitor for each room watched by two guards, twenty-four-seven,' Reid said. 'These are VIPs — Very Important Prisoners — understood?'

'Understood,' the man answered.

11

'Good news, Bob,' Ralph told Robert when he stopped by his home and office to check on the progress of the repairs. 'As soon as the government contractors finish the security upgrades and the building inspector gives his okay, you can move back in.'

'Sounds great, Ralph,' Robert replied. 'When do you think it'll be ready?'

'You should be certified by Friday, and can begin moving in over the weekend.' Ralph smiled as he informed his friend. 'You've got plenty of offers to help get everything done.'

* * *

On Thursday, the government security people had finished installing all of the special security alarms and telephone lines that would allegedly prevent another break-in. Even the garage entries had been secured.

'My desktop and peripherals are ready for pick-up,' Robert told them. 'I can get them and return in forty-five minutes. We can install your security codes and my new anti-intrusion software as soon as I get back.'

After the internet detective returned, he began installing his new equipment. As each part of the new system was hooked up to the electrical and other connections, the security people installed the government-level protection files.

'We can include your laptop in this security umbrella,' the lead technician advised. 'The WiFi version is the best security measure written to date.'

'When we've included my new invasion firewall,' Robert commented, 'I should be well protected. Thank you.'

'Be sure to get a copyright on that software,' the second security person told him. 'That could prove to be a nice little nest-egg income. Computer companies would pay good money for nearly unbreakable security codes.'

'Just as soon as it's proven in the field.'

On Friday, the building inspector checked Robert's refurbished and upgraded home and office, and also checked the building plans. After verifying that everything was up to, and even above, the building code requirements, he signed the certification papers.

'You can move back into the building at any time.' The inspector smiled as he shook Robert's hand. 'I'm glad that everything went as smoothly and as quickly as it did. Good luck.'

'Thank you. It feels good to be back in my own place again.'

*   *   *

After all of his friends had finished helping him put all of his home and office furniture back into their proper places, and agreed to return for breakfast the following morning, Robert booted up his new system and replaced all of his programs and files. He then loaded in the new software he had written and began to search for Amerindian dream symbols. While he found references to spiders, he found nothing about paraplegic spiders controlling an intricate web from a chair, as other spiders caught many flies for it. Sighing in frustration, Robert widened his search to include symbolic dream spiders from other cultures.

'All of those traders intermarrying into all of those other cultures over so many generations have made for an interesting mixture of symbols,' he muttered to himself. 'No wonder my dreams are so hard to understand.'

After some more futile searching, and a jaw-cracking yawn, Robert decided to check all of his new security locks and go to bed. 'Wake me if you need to go out tonight,' he told Mr. Dog. 'Tomorrow we'll work on teaching you the new routine for letting yourself out.'

The night passed without incident, and morning found Robert well rested and ready to tackle the problem of hunting the IP address of the code that had invaded the Federal Reserve Bank and the government's secret project accounts.

* * *

The government technicians returned just after the midday meal to fine-tune the new security systems.

'Everything seems to be in top working order,' the lead tech reported with a smile. 'How's your private security software integrating with ours?'

'So far everything seems to mesh smoothly,' Robert said. 'There haven't been any real tests of either program yet, so I'll just have wait and see. I still need to teach my dog how to use the noseprint reader to let himself in and out. That shouldn't take long.'

'Smart dog?'

'And well-motivated,' was the answer. 'I found him when he was around eight weeks old. Starved, mistreated, and with several injuries. I cleaned him up and took him to the vet. The doc gave him some meds for his cuts and bruises, a deworming treatment, and a flea dip. I fed and comforted him, showed him love, and eventually I was able to win his trust. He'll do almost anything for me.'

'Unconditional love,' said the other tech. 'Not easily won from an animal that was mistreated so young.'

'Why have two security programs?' the first tech asked. 'Why the redundancy?'

Robert thought about his answer for a moment before he replied. 'If I could find a third, or even a fourth, as good as these two, I'd add them as well. Very often, one program will find a problem that another will miss. Both of these programs have been designed as hunter/killer programs. They'll hunt down a program that infects the system and eliminate it. However, while the government uses recognition technology to eliminate dangerous codes, I designed my program to hunt down and capture any foreign code and sterilize it before it reaches the hard drive. Sort of combining White Man's technology with Red Man's magic and mythology. Between the two, I believe they'll protect my computers from about ninety percent of all malicious attacks.'

'What about tracking the attack back to its source?' the lead tech wanted to know.

'I based that bit of software on the way hunters and trackers have always followed their prey,' Robert answered. 'All of the small things that even the best can miss when they try to hide their trail. One can't think of everything during the hunt, whether they're the hunted or the hunter. But the more one knows, the better it is for him.'

As the technicians wrapped up their work, Agents Shirley Reid and James Black parked in an empty space in front of the pharmacy across the street.

'We've been assigned to your protection detail for the duration, by order of the President,' Agent Black said as he and Agent Reid walked into Moonsinger's office. 'Apparently Agent Sorenz liked your no-nonsense attitude when you were first interviewed. Now the President is adamant that these people must not only be stopped, but that their infiltration abilities are neutralized — as permanently as possible. He's convinced that you have the best shot at what he wants.'

12

The Boss was red-faced with anger. 'What do you mean, 'Tsunami' was compromised?' he yelled into his desk phone. 'That program was designed to send the information to a secure system and completely wipe out anything that could be traced back to us from the internet! How did Moonsinger stop the process?'

'He designed his own sniffer/capture program,' the person on the other end of the conversation replied. 'It's like nothing our people have seen before. It not only finds and identifies suspect programs, but it also tags them without any way to trace the tag back to its source.'

'Moonsinger is more of a danger than I realized,' the Boss growled. 'I want him and that dog of his terminated — with extreme prejudice. Then I want all of his security programs, files, and codes copied before they're erased totally and irretrievably.'

Slamming the receiver down, he yelled for his manservant.

'Michael!' he said as he wheeled away from his desk. 'Prepare the car. We need to go to the secure site.'

★   ★   ★

The nondescript warehouse was in the poorest of the industrial areas of Sandfield. Michael used a remote control to open the large door and drove inside. The interior's ultra-modern and high-tech equipment belied the exterior's decrepitude. On arrival, he helped his boss exit the car and placed him in his wheelchair. Together they made their way to the large office.

'Show me what portions of the plans 'Tsunami' was unable to eliminate,' the Boss ordered. 'I want to know exactly how effective the enemy's countermeasures were and what information he now has. I also want all of our operations moved to the fourth-place sites. Don't bother with the secondary and tertiary sites. The enemy may already know about them and be planning his moves against them. I want 'Operation Scorched Earth' activated immediately! On all of the primary, secondary, and tertiary sites!'

'Scorched Earth' has already begun on the primary sites,' the man in charge of the warehouse said. 'We can begin on the secondary and tertiary sites in less than ten minutes. Some things have already been moved to those sites and will have to be removed.'

'Leave them in place,' the Boss ordered forcefully. 'It'll give authenticity to our plans.'

'But what about the data?' the warehouse leader wondered. 'Won't it be lost to 'Scorched Earth'?'

'They've already been blind-copied,' Michael reported, 'and made ready for reinstallation at the quaternary sites.'

'You've used up two of your ten minutes,' the Boss commented. 'You'd better start moving, or you'll be left behind as a warning against displeasing me.'

The alarms sounded; orders were issued; everything not already transferred was left onsite; everything else was detoured to the new sites. The change of plans was fully implemented with seconds to spare.

★   ★   ★

Robert checked his computer for any fresh developments while his first pot of coffee was brewing. He was hoping that he would have something new to tell his clients.

The coffee maker was noisily making its finishing efforts as Agents Reid and Black walked into his office. 'The coffee's just finishing,' he told them as he gestured for them to have a seat. 'I was just checking what my programs may have discovered overnight.'

Robert poured three cups of coffee, set two before the agents, and then sat back behind his desk. He clicked a few keys and manipulated his mouse once or twice before sitting back with a puzzled look on his face. 'Our birds have flown,' he commented blandly, 'and have left very little of value behind. They apparently abandoned three main sets of secure sites in a virtual 'Scorched Earth' configuration.'

'Would they have transferred all of their data to a fourth set of secure sites?' Black inquired.

'Most people would believe that three places to run to would give them plenty of places to hide while they rebuilt their forces,' Robert replied. 'What I think is that they planned not only a fourth escape route, but possibly a fifth — or even a sixth — way out of being caught.'

As the Secret Service agents sipped their coffee and looked on, Robert busied himself writing a program, checking its progress, and either frowning or looking relieved according to its success. After several minutes, he looked up at his allies and let out a sigh filled with exhaustion and mild satisfaction.

'They've moved their data to a fourth set of secure sites,' he told them. 'This time, they've managed to put in several blind trails to hide their true place — or places — of hiding. It may take a while to locate the new real-world safe house.'

'Can you estimate how long?' Shirley Reid asked.

'Maybe just an hour,' came the distracted reply, 'maybe a day, or even a week. It all depends on who's the better hacker.'

★   ★   ★

Robert worked with his pet, teaching the dog a new routine for letting himself in and out during the night, or those times when Robert had to leave him alone while checking clues or evidence in the real world. Even with all of the updated security measures, the dog was the best last line of defense.

'That's right, fella,' Robert encouraged the animal, 'just place your nose against the lighted box. When the light goes off, you can go through the door. You do the same thing going out or coming in.'

Mr. Dog looked at Robert, and then at the box next to his place of ingress and egress. He placed his nose near the box to sniff at the light. As his nose touched the box during his curious scrutiny, the door swung open and the animal went outside. The door automatically closed after fifteen seconds. When the dog satisfied himself that his backyard had no unwanted visitors, he returned to his doggy-door.

Unsure how he had opened the door to go out, the canine began to try several things without success until his attention was drawn to the box with the light. Once again, he sniffed the new device next to his door. When the door opened, he quickly passed through and gave a self-satisfied bark.

'Figured it out now, did you?' he heard Robert say as he scratched the animal's ears in praise and reward. 'I think just a couple of more times and you'll have the new routine down pat. Let's lock up and go to the dog park.'

Grabbing the leash from its hook and attaching it to the canine's collar, he set the alarm system and took Mr. Dog to the park where he could stretch his legs. An hour and a half later, Robert gave a three-note whistle to let the dog know that it was time to go home.

'Playtime's over,' he said when his pet responded to the call. 'Time to go back to work.'

Attaching the leash back on the collar, Robert enjoyed the pleasant afternoon weather as they walked back home. It wouldn't be long before the summer arrived, Robert thought as they admired the flowering hedge of a neighbor. Then it would start to get too hot for these long walks until dusk.

*   *   *

As Robert and his dog walked along the sidewalks, they failed to notice that they were under surreptitious surveillance from the occupants of a dark tan work van.

'Subjects headed back toward home,' the man in the passenger seat said into his handheld microphone. 'No sign of any bodyguards. Initiate 'Wipeout' plan, Alpha-red-two.'

Using an especially sensitive 'shotgun' pick-up microphone, the two federal agents also watching the man and dog

113

conferred together.

'I don't like our protectee allowing himself to be bait for drawing his attackers out into the open this way,' Shirley confessed to James, 'but I've got to admit that it seems to be working.'

'Our bird is on the wing,' James said as the people in the work van started its engine and moved into traffic.

'All units,' Shirley reported by radio to the other agents, 'threat to subject is on the move. They've initiated their plan.'

James started his car and followed the van as the undercover agents moved in closer so as to be ready when their opponents did whatever it was that they had planned.

The work van did not approach Robert and his dog as it had been expected to do. Instead, it drove a couple of blocks past them, and then turned right at that intersection before turning left to follow a parallel course toward Robert's residence.

'All units,' Shirley reported, 'threat to subject now following parallel route of subject. Be alert for any aggressive action.'

James continued to follow the van for a few more blocks.

'I think we've been fooled,' he observed, 'if they're using themselves as a diversion — '

Just then, the van did a very sharp U-turn and accelerated past the agents.

'What the devil?' Shirley exclaimed. 'We've been suckered!'

James did his best imitation of a bootlegger being pursued by ATF agents as he also did a tight U-turn, while Agent Reid notified their teammates and the police of the current situation.

Agent Black turned on his red and blue lights as the siren wailed in his pursuit of the van. The van must have had an illegally powerful engine, because it was able to pull away from the federal cruiser. James saw the van's tail-lights as it turned toward the route that Robert and his dog were taking.

'Threat van headed toward subject,' Shirley reported excitedly into her radio. 'Unknown type of action. Extra-powerful engine. Put air pursuit into play.'

As the agents headed toward where

they expected the van to be going, other attackers came out of hiding, using a form of sleep gas on their intended victims and anyone nearby or attempting to approach them. As Robert collapsed, and the dog tried valiantly to keep the assailants away from his master before he was also overcome, the van screeched to a halt. Robert was hastily picked up, and all of the kidnappers got into the van through the open sliding door. As soon as everyone had gotten in and the door was slid closed, the vehicle left the area with its tires billowing smoke — leaving the dog and the agents behind.

By the time Reid and Black arrived, the van was just pulling out of sight. The gassed agents and the dog were starting to return to consciousness as the paramedics and the local police arrived.

'The chopper just got in the air,' one of the police officers reported. 'They should be able to spot them quickly.'

'Let's hope that they can,' a frustrated Agent Black said. 'This was too well-planned for there not to be someone on the inside. We need to have that person found — preferably yesterday, if not sooner.'

'The planning sessions were kept pretty tight,' Detective Brown offered. 'They were held at Moonsinger's office with only you, me, Agent Reid, Detective Smith, and the supporting agents the only ones at the meeting. Do you suspect one of them? Or do you think a listening device was used?'

'There are fairly sophisticated ways to listen in on people without planting electronic listening units inside the room or building,' James replied. 'I don't see any of our people or the agents being spies for the opposition. You, me, and all of our people have been well vetted for this detail.'

13

As Robert began to regain his senses, he became aware that he was blindfolded, gagged, and bound. He hoped that the contingency plans that he and Agents Reid and Black had secretly made had not been discovered. The subcutaneous tracking device had been an afterthought, and had been hoped to be an unnecessary safety net.

'He's waking up,' a male voice to his right said.

'Make sure that all of the restraints are secure,' a voice from the front seat replied. 'The Boss won't be pleased if he escapes and finds his way back to his office.'

The person to Robert's left roughly checked his gag, hand and foot restraints, and the safety harness.

'He's as snug as a bug in a rug,' he told the people in front.

'You're sure that everyone was out

when we picked you up?' the other voice up front asked.

'Even the dog was sleeping like a baby,' the man was told.

'That cop car was pretty close on our tail.' The front passenger's voice sounded concerned. 'They had that police chopper in the area right fast. You barely evaded them.'

'Yeah, the Boss's idea to hide in the storm channel underpass was probably our salvation,' the driver agreed. 'Good thing we got into place before they caught up with us.'

'The Boss likes to plan for the unexpected,' the man on Robert's right said. 'That's why he's always three or four steps ahead of anyone else.'

Robert listened to his captors' chatter and stored it in his memory for future reference. Everything that they revealed about the person in charge was one more clue to finding the missing money and the purloined documents. He needed all of the information he could gather to find out what was being planned for their use.

After an indeterminate time for Robert, the van was brought to a halt. The men got out, hauling him inside a chilly interior. He thought that he was possibly in an underground cave or a building kept at a slightly uncomfortable temperature. The place must have either been lined with soundproofing, or built to avoid any hint of an echo.

Robert was made to sit in a chair as his blindfold and gag were removed. In front of him was an old-fashioned utility desk. A man who sat behind it that reminded him of his dream spider.

'You've been quite troublesome, Mr. Moonsinger,' the man's hard-edged voice told him. 'It'll give me great satisfaction to cause you unendurable pain while I extract how you were able to defeat all of my best programmers' intrusion and malware countermeasures.'

'Any talented programmer with hunter and tracking instincts could have followed your internet trail,' Robert offered blandly. 'All it took was a little determined effort, some perseverance, and lots of the aptitude to win.'

'But now,' the man behind the desk sneered, 'it would seem that my aptitude for winning is stronger than yours — my determination greater.'

'That still remains to be seen.'

'Ah,' the Boss remarked, 'but you're the one sitting bound to a chair — helpless to counter any demand of you I make.'

'Again,' Robert repeated, 'that remains to be seen.'

Two large men with cold dead eyes entered the room when the Boss pressed a buzzer built into his desk. After receiving instructions to take Robert to the information extraction room, they picked him up and carried him to a cell without windows and an uncomfortable chair bolted to the floor.

'You'll be fastened to the chair until the Boss says he has no further use for you,' the bigger of the two men told him, fastening restraints around his wrists, ankles, chest, and hips. 'These can only be unlocked with the Boss's special key. You can forget any notion of getting yourself free.'

As the last restraint was snapped into

place, the smaller man reared back his fist and punched Robert in the pit of his stomach. 'Payback for what your dog did to my cousin at the motel,' he growled.

* * *

'Do we have a clear signal?' Agent Sorenz asked. 'Can we track it to its source?'

The woman looking at the flashing dot on the electronic map of Sandfield and the two-mile circumference surrounding it glanced up as she answered. 'It's a very strong signal, sir.'

'Are we ready to go?' Rick asked the leader of his special Hostage Rescue Team. 'I made a promise to that man, and I intend to expend every effort to keep it.'

'Five minutes to pass orders and mount up,' the team leader reported.

'Any news on how the perps knew what our plans were?' Sorenz questioned.

'We found a tiny transmitter at the lower corner of Moonsinger's big picture window. It was embedded in what appeared to be a speck of dust. And its signal was hard to detect,' the electronics expert told him as she gazed at the map.

'Have the men and his dog fully recovered?'

'Yes, sir,' the lead man informed Sorenz. 'Dr. Ward has taken the animal in until we find and release Moonsinger. I don't think his pet will be trusting of very many people just now.'

'I think maybe we should take the mutt along,' a second man opined. 'He could find Moonsinger once we locate and enter the building where he's being held.'

'And taking the mutt along,' Sorenz said with a grin, 'just might limit the damage to the vet's kennels and office. Shirley! James! The dog knows and trusts you the best. Pick him up at the vet's and meet us here. He pointed to a spot two blocks from where Moonsinger's tracker had stopped.

With that, the six men and two women headed toward their vehicles and prepared to travel.

'Everyone follow Joyce and me,' Rick instructed. 'That way, if Robert's moved, no one gets lost. Shirley, if the rendezvous changes, we'll find a way to let you know.'

★ ★ ★

As Michael wheeled his boss into the room, Robert was reminded of the spider in his dreams that could not use the lower half of its legs. What his spirit had revealed in these dreams was now becoming clear. Just like that iconic detective from the late nineteenth century had remarked about his nemesis, he thought — a spider at the center of its web, controlling its empire!

The two men with dead eyes and practiced stoicism placed themselves behind Michael and their boss. Their hands were now gloved in flexible but hard boiled-leather coverings. Their arms were almost as big as Moonsinger's thighs.

'I'll ask the questions,' the Boss told him, 'and if I don't like your answers, or you fail to respond, these 'ungentlemen' will practice their boxing skills on you. Do I make myself clear?'

'Go to hell!'

One of the men stepped forward, cocked back a fist, and punched Robert just above his beltline. Gasping for breath, Robert's glare promised retribution.

'I asked if I'd made myself clear,' the Boss repeated when Robert had recovered enough breath to answer.

'Very clear,' Robert replied, 'but it won't do you any good if I don't know the answer.'

'You'll be given three chances to remember. Then one of my men will break a bone. Nothing serious, just very painful, I assure you.'

Robert had been questioned for what had felt to him like an eternity when alarm klaxons began to wail.

'Take care of him,' the Boss ordered. 'I don't want him killed, just incapacitated. That'll give us time to go to ground.'

Michael wheeled his master out of the room as the enforcers began a thorough beating of their victim.

The Boss and his other minions exited through secret tunnels and pathways to waiting vehicles, and began to scatter to the four winds as the entrance was breached. Nearly a dozen armed and determined men and women efficiently immobilized those who were too slow in making their escapes.

Mr. Dog quickly found Moonsinger's spoor, and led Reid and Black — along with Sorenz, Joyce, and several agents — down a long hallway. There, they heard the solid thunks of armored fists hammering flesh. The animal crashed into the room, teeth bared and an angry growl in his throat.

So intent were the men who were beating Robert that they didn't know they were under attack until the dog had leaped on one of them and was biting the back of his victim's neck. With a scream of pain and terror, the man tried to cover his head and roll away from the fury of his attacker. Reid placed the barrel of her weapon against the other man's temple.

'Freeze, or end up missing your favorite head!' she ordered.

'Get him offa me!' the man that Mr. Dog had down screamed. '*Get this monster offa me!*'

It took six people to hold the frenzied dog while the prisoners were taken into custody. When they were gone, the dog was released and immediately bounded to Robert, who was unconscious by the time his restraints were cut away from the chair. His pet began whining and licking Robert's face.

'Get him into my car,' Rick ordered. 'Call the hospital and tell them that we have a seriously injured man coming in.'

Robert was carefully transported to Sorenz's car. Along with the dog, two people got into the back seat to hold Robert in place. Sorenz sped toward the hospital with full siren blaring and the lights flashing.

★   ★   ★

'Most of our people were able to get away safely,' the Boss was told. 'None of the others allowed themselves to be captured alive. They all died fighting.'

'How were these agents and the police able to find our location?' The Boss's lack of expression sent a deathly chill through the man he was talking to. 'No one should have been able to connect that building with any surreptitious or illegal activities.'

'We expected to have plenty of time for you to interrogate that PI and to get the place cleaned of all evidence before they realized Moonsinger had been there.'

'So,' the Boss queried, 'how did they find us? I want the head of the incompetent who fouled up.'

'That person is as good as found, sir,' the assistant assured him.

14

Robert Moonsinger awakened, feeling groggy and in pain. As he tossed in his bed, he felt a warm, wet tongue caress his fingers and realized that his most faithful friend was with him — wherever he was.

'Hey, fella,' he greeted the animal that was now returning his greeting with glad whining and thumping tail. 'Did they allow you in the hospital room with me? Well, however it happened, I'm glad you're here.'

'The hospital staff didn't want to allow it, but he kept finding his way into your room. The second time, he refused to be removed — very emphatically — so the staff decided it was better to let him stay. He hasn't left your side except to take call-of-nature breaks in over a day and half.' The voice was that of Rick Sorenz of the Secret Service. 'I promised that you wouldn't end up as a sacrificial lamb,' he added. 'I keep my promises.'

'That's twice,' Robert said with a grin as he scratched Mr. Dog's ears, 'that the US Cavalry has charged to my rescue. Count me among those who are grateful for your excellent timing.'

'Mr. Dog was included in the rescue when the tracker stopped moving,' Robert was informed. 'He led us to where you were playing the part of a human punching bag. One of your two playmates is here in the prison ward recovering from the damage done to him by your 'Special and Private' protection detail.

Mr. Dog contentedly acknowledged the attention being given him from the Secret Service man.

'Since you're in good hands — er, paws — I'll let your doctor know that you're definitely awake,' Rick said and left the room.

Minutes later, a hospital resident and Dr. Ward entered the room. Mr. Dog perked up at the sight of his vet.

'How's my favorite patient?' Dr. Ward asked pleasantly as he attached Mr. Dog's leash. 'Let's take a walk while Dr. Kyle checks out your friend. Besides, you look hungry. You wouldn't want to pass out on watch, would you?'

Mr. Dog looked up at Robert, who said, 'Go with Dr. Ward, boy. I'll be all right until the two of you get back.'

With a look and a sharp bark that seemed to indicate 'If you say so,' Mr. Dog allowed himself to be led from the room.

Once they left, Dr. Kyle remarked, 'Your pet's been very protective since you were brought in battered into unresponsiveness. Dr. Ward was the only person he'd pay any attention to. After we took care of your abrasions, bruises, etcetera, Dr. Ward brought him into the recovery room. The dog seemed okay with you having been sedated, but wouldn't leave your bedside. After Dr. Ward and two orderlies were finally able to coax him outside, he kept sneaking back into the hospital, searching for you. The second time he found you, he *absolutely* refused to be removed. It was either let him stay or take the chance of injury to him or to other parties. We let him stay. Agents Sorenz, Reid and Black all vouched for the dog's behavior, as did Dr. Ward. After that, he's been as well-behaved as any model visitor.'

'He's been that way since I found him dumped in an alley as a puppy,' Robert replied. 'He'd been badly injured and malnourished. Dr. Ward treated his wounds, and I provided lots of TLC.'

★ ★ ★

When Robert was released — against medical advice — from the hospital and allowed to return home, Mr. Dog kept an attentive eye on him. Agents Reid, Black and Sorenz made sure that Robert didn't overtax himself.

'What did the leader look like?' Sorenz asked. 'Did you get a good look at anyone else?'

Robert described the Boss and his physical limitations in great detail. 'He acted like some spider controlling an intricate web — pulling strings first here, then there.' Robert gave his impression of the set-up as he had observed it. 'Each section, in turn, had a smaller spider doing his bidding. Every minion had his job to do, and was totally responsible to the boss. If he failed, he was eliminated and replaced. It appeared to be an intricate system of fear and reward.'

After Robert had checked all of the security locks and retired for the evening, the agents discussed what they had recently learned.

'We now know that the 'New Internet Agency' is believed to be a front run by a paraplegic Eurasian only known as 'the Boss',' Sorenz said. 'His reputation up to now has been that of a highly respectable and successful internet businessman. No one seems to know how he got his original backing, but he's managed to multiply his wealth many times over.'

'Any indication of using hostile take-over techniques to acquire other businesses?' Shirley inquired thoughtfully.

'None that the FBI and the SEC have been able to verify,' Rick answered. 'The Boss has a layer of legal eagles to protect his reputation, and has always seemed to have good relations with nearly all of both his former and current competitors.'

'So,' James said, 'no one has a discouraging word to say about the man?'

'Apparently not,' Sorenz answered with a shrug. 'Either he's as good as he appears, or he's cowed all of his enemies thoroughly.'

James skimmed through the New Internet Agency's business prospectus and history as he remarked, 'It seems that the Eurasian's company has been in the habit of acquiring programmers and hackers specializing in internet protection and intrusion programs. Maybe the kinds of things Moonsinger has been running into.'

'And possibly the kinds of things that would be both attractive and dangerous to the Eurasian's plans,' Shirley agreed.

'Look into it,' Sorenz said.

15

The Sandfield offices of the New Internet Agency were located on the fourth floor of the Virtual Businesses and Cybernet Jobs building in the downtown business district. Shelly Brown, Shirley Reid, and an independent computer expert who often freelanced for the Sandfield police had met a block away to discuss their plans.

'Everybody know the parts they'll play?' Shirley asked.

'I go in ahead of the two of you,' Pete, the computer expert, spoke first, 'and apply for a position as a software writer, and act the way a total computer nerd would. I'm looking for anything that might possibly be related to the illegal use of the internet. While I'm there, I'll try to get any hand-outs about the company.'

'Try to get a feel for employee enthusiasm, loyalty, and anything else that seems important or off,' Shirley responded. 'Shelly and I will come in asking to check the business licenses. We'll say we're doing random checks because of possible trouble that we can't disclose at this time. Agent Aguirre will have one of his agents get with us before we go in who'll be making noises about national security.'

'And I'm your local liaison,' Shelly added. 'I think that we have the plan as well thought out as possible. As soon as Agent Aguirre's representative arrives and is checked out, we'll get started.'

Agent Richards from Homeland Security arrived minutes later. He identified himself, showed his credentials, and spoke the proper code phrase. Everyone was given last-minute instructions, and Pete went inside the Virtual Businesses and Cybernet Jobs building and took the elevator to the fourth floor.

The outer office was among the largest and plushest that Pete had ever been in. The male secretary was dressed in an expensive modern but conservative blue suit with a white silk shirt and lemon-yellow tie. 'May I help you?' he asked as Pete walked in.

'I'm here to inquire about your requirements for programmers,' he informed the man.

'I've been self-employed successfully for three years. Competition from big companies like this one has made me rethink my attitude toward my livelihood.'

'What sort of work do you do, Mr . . . ?'

'Thorton,' Pete replied. 'Pete Thorton. I'm a specialist in security programming.'

'What areas of security programming has your work been related to?'

'Intrusion prevention, firewall upgrades, and anything related to keeping out unwanted hackers.'

'Let me check with human resources while you fill out our questionnaire. If you have a résumé, you can attach it.'

The secretary used the interoffice phone for a few minutes while Pete filled out the questionnaire. As he hung up the phone, he told Pete, 'Mr. Rush will see you as soon as you've filled out the form. He just had a cancellation, and so he has time for an interview now.'

'Thank you,' Pete replied as he picked

up his briefcase and gave the secretary back his clipboard and pen.

The secretary escorted Pete to Mr. Rush's door and announced him. After the amenities, Pete gave Mr. Rush his résumé and the filled-out questionnaire and took the offered chair. 'Thank you for seeing me on such short notice,' he said in his most polite tone.

'One of our clients is looking into some highly specialized safety measures, Mr. Thorton,' Mr. Rush said as he skimmed over the résumé and question-naire. 'I see that you have a couple of copyrights on your work. Could you summarize their purpose and overall effectiveness, please?'

Pete gave a precise synopsis of the copyrighted programs and the effective-ness rating given by the clients who had used them for about fifteen minutes, after which, Rush asked pertinent questions intended to check whether or not Pete was what he claimed to be.

'I think,' Rush told Thorton after half an hour of intense interrogation, 'that you may have the skills that our client's looking for. Because of the nature of the work, you must understand our need to do a thorough background check. As soon as that's been completed to our satisfaction, we'll contact you for a starting date.'

'I'm sure that everything will be satisfactory,' Pete replied with self-assurance. 'However, will I be notified if anything is amiss?'

'Only to inform you that you did not meet our needs at this time, Mr. Thorton. Our assessments are strictly confidential and will not be revealed to any other prospective employer to whom you may wish to apply.'

They shook hands and Pete left the office. Underneath the visitor's chair, Pete had left an almost invisibly small voice-activated micro-transmitter he had been given. The device was not only hard to spot, but because it transmitted on an ultra-low frequency, it was unlikely that the signal would be detected during a security sweep.

★ ★ ★

Pete Thorton met with Agent Reid and Detective Brown outside a local coffee shop. 'I think I was given the standard 'Don't call us. We'll call you' routine,' he told them. 'I'm not sure he fully accepted my cover story, but at least I don't believe that I grew any tails when I left.'

'Waterman's watchdogs told me that you were clean when you left the building and that they didn't see any signs of suspicious characters for at least the first block,' Reid informed him just as her cell phone demanded her attention. She checked and saw that she'd received a text from one of Matisha's operatives.

'Agent Waterman's people have checked your vehicle,' she reported when she'd read the message. 'It appears to be clean. Either you haven't been made, or they wish to investigate you further.'

'All of the back-ups for my cover were supposed to have been in place before I went in,' Pete said.

''Supposed to have been' being the operative term.'

★　★　★

A nervous Mr. Rush was on the phone with the Boss. 'I think the opposition is suspicious,' he said. 'A man was in my office not an hour ago asking for a programmer position in our internet security department.'

'Have you checked him out yet?' the Boss wished to know.

'The preliminary work all says that he's what he claims, but I'm having his background checked more thoroughly.'

'Good. Keep me informed.' The Boss waited a beat, and then added, 'Eliminate him if you're not 100% sure.'

'And if I am?'

'Then hire him, but don't give him anything sensitive until he's proven himself. We need some new blood.'

The Boss nervously stroked his clean-shaven chin after he disconnected. Too many things were going wrong. Operatives who had previously performed well were making intolerable mistakes, security walls that were supposed to be unbreachable were failing, and people were sniffing at things that they were supposed to be unaware of.

He had too much time and too many resources committed to this project to just pull out and walk away. The potential return was too enticing.

Michael came in and announced, 'The Brakeman is on line three, sir.'

'Thank you Michael.'

The Brakeman succinctly gave his report, and the Boss began to relax a bit. At last, something was going as planned. The transfers of all of the computer files and programs had been done without any tell-tales piggy-backed on them. He was certain now that he now had enough breathing room to finish this project and disappear without a trace. He had had a good run; but the way this job had kept fouling up, he thought that it was time to retire. No one succeeded in this business forever, and very few left the game alive.

★   ★   ★

Robert was sitting at his desk checking the tracking programs on the money trail that had been the start of this danger-ously frustrating case. Every time that he got close to his prey, the bait would be taken and he would need to discover a new trail to find his quarry.

The current trail had all but disappeared. The faint indications of the transfer of funds gave him hope, if fleeting, that he had at last found where the pilfered monies were now placed. He was busy writing a vicious program that would remove the funds from their illegal locations and return them to their proper accounts.

'Impossible' was not an acceptable part of his vocabulary when referring to enemy programming and counteracting it.

'Now,' he said to Mr. Dog, 'let's see what reaction we get when our villainous programmers find their funds have been electronically erased.' Mr. Dog gave him his best doggy grin.

After checking on the retransfer of the funds, Robert removed all traces of his intrusion to prevent his adversaries from reversing the transfer. He also placed an alarm and tracking file with the returned funds.

'Try to get away with the money now,'

he said with a grin.

'Someone looks like the cat that swallowed the last goldfish,' Detective Shelly Brown remarked as she walked into the office of Moonsinger's Internet Investigations.

'Yeah,' added her partner, 'who did you snare for us?'

'Just a few internet thieves,' Moonsinger replied. 'I just stole back a ton of pilfered funds and placed it back where it belonged. If the thieves try it again, we'll know and will be able to trace the theft back to our perpetrators.'

'You're sure it'll work?' Brown quizzed.

'As sure as one can be,' he replied, 'with the internet.'

★   ★   ★

'What do you mean, the funds are gone?' The Eurasian's features looked as if he were having a heart attack, his face was so red.

'The money is no longer in our special accounts,' the CFO reported. 'It's almost as if they were never there!'

'Find those missing funds and get them back!' The Boss was not safely to be trifled with when in such a state. 'And place extra security on the prototype! Our business is as good as dead if we can't deliver!'

The CFO hurriedly left his volcanic boss's office, mumbling assurances that the funds would be recovered.

It had to be that unmentionable data hunter! He had been a thorn in the side — a burr under the saddle — ever since he had become involved in his affairs. No one could be allowed to interfere with his plans the way Robert Moonsinger had.

The Boss flipped a switch on his desk intercom. 'Get me our best exterminators,' he said. 'I have a very persistent pest that needs to be permanently removed.' He was through being Mr. Nice Guy.

*　*　*

'It looks as if Pete Thorton has outlived his usefulness,' Shirley Reid remarked after she heard the recording of Mr. Rush's telephone conversation with his boss. 'For his own safety, have Shelly reassign him.'

'Yes, ma'am.'

That avenue was no longer of assistance to Robert Moonsinger; it had just been blocked. As Reid contemplated her next move, another aide came into her office.

'Ma'am,' he said, 'the New Internet Agency is shutting down. Everything is being packed up, and movers are on their way.'

'What the . . . ?' Juan Aguirre spluttered beside her.

'A man came into Rush's office and gave orders to close up shop, code word 'Scorched Earth'.'

'Have the FBI alerted, and let's get our own people in place,' Aguirre ordered. 'I don't want them getting away. They'll just turn up again, better prepared next time.'

The building was surrounded within the hour, and even then, the net was thrown out too late. By the time the various federal agents entered the offices on the fourth floor, there was not a person or a stick of furniture left to seize or capture.

'They may have slipped through our fingers this time,' Agent Black said, 'but they're obviously running scared.'

*　*　*

'There was nothing left in their suite of offices?' Robert asked when he heard the news.

'Not even the micro-transmitter Pete left behind,' the special agent from the FBI told him. 'Even the carpets had been vacuumed clean. The place was as bare as Old Mother Hubbard's cupboard.'

'From what you told me,' Robert said thoughtfully, 'our suspects bugged out of their offices shortly after I transferred their stolen funds back to where they belonged. I'd say that the two events were definitely related.'

'I agree,' the agent replied. 'But where have they hidden themselves?'

'Until they get their money back,' Moonsinger thought out loud, 'they probably won't go far. And they still have to find a buyer for the military prototype.'

'As quickly as we made our raid,' the agent commented, 'they must have had their escape plan in place for some time. They always seem to be half-a-jump ahead of us.'

'Can we get extra security around Bob and his dog?' Shelly asked both the FBI agent and Agent Reynolds. 'They've got to know who removed their funds.'

'The agents from Sorenz's department are being augmented with two full teams of highly vetted teams who are expert in covert and high visibility protection,' Agent Reynolds replied. 'The enemy's agents would have to have the mythical abilities of Ninja warriors to get close to Mr. Moonsinger and his canine partner.'

'If they do have those skills,' Shelly added, 'I for one wouldn't care to tally the body count.'

No further comment was made. All present showed grim faces.

★ ★ ★

The exterminator team stood at attention before the Eurasian man in his motorized wheelchair. The leader of the team had been given a dossier packet and now they were being given their instructions.

'I don't care how you take care of this pest,' the Boss elaborated. 'No need to be fancy or attempt to send a message. The death of the target, alone, should do that. Any and all collateral damages will be acceptable, as the target is believed to be highly protected. Don't allow anyone to get in your way.'

The team turned as one and left the presence of their benefactor.

'They'd better succeed,' the Boss uttered to himself as his specialized team of exterminators disappeared, 'or they'd better not return to face my wrath. The Moonsinger Internet Investigations Agency is proving to be too competent for its own good. Or for the health of my business.'

The man wheeled back to his desk and began pecking at the keyboard of his computer. He had a lot to accomplish before the day's work was done.

'Moonsinger was able to retrieve the missing monies and put them back into their proper accounts,' Agent Shirley Reid reported to Rick Sorenz, her boss at the Secret Service agency. 'But so far, he only knows that the prototype weapon hasn't been placed on the black market yet. He believes that because of the sensitivity of the product, the people who stole the plans may be waiting for the right buyer to indicate an interest in new weapons technology before announcing its availability.'

'It's a possibility,' Agent Sorenz agreed. 'However, we haven't the luxury for the first move to be made by someone else. The chance that someone else getting the technology before we can implement it, also making it obsolete, would be devastating to our national defenses.'

'Moonsinger has a solid lead that he is following up on, based on what he believes he learned during his kidnapping,' Agent Reid told him. 'The FBI also gave him some tentative information gained from the men who gave him his beating.'

'By the way,' Rick inquired, 'how are his injuries? I understand that the attack was brutal.'

'The doctors all say,' Shirley replied, 'that he should still be in the hospital. He insisted on checking himself out against medical advice and is working from his office. James and his pet, Mr. Dog, are with him constantly as he works. The two protection details assigned to him. James, Agent Reynolds, an FBI agent and I also take shifts watching Robert's back, while Pete Thorton watches the Internet's back door.'

16

While Agents Reid and Sorenz were having their discussion, Robert Moonsinger and Sally were having a different type of discussion at the diner.

'The past few weeks have certainly been newsy,' Sally said as she placed Robert's order on the counter. 'First your place gets broken into and an attempt at arson is made, then you get kidnapped and beaten, and now there are all kinds of out-of-towners near and in your office and home. Must be a pretty interesting case you've got, Bob. At least that's what everybody who comes in here is saying.'

'Just keep what you hear between you and me, Sal.' Moonsinger said with concern in his voice. 'Right now, things are getting rough. Be careful who you talk to and how you react to what you hear. Let me know about any strangers who seem to know too much about what's going down over at my place, or are too nosey about my agency. I don't want you getting hurt.'

'Hey,' Sally said with a grin, 'it's been a long time since we were what used to be called 'an item,' you know.'

'These creeps aren't the types who care anything about that, if they think that they can use you to get to me. Just knowing that we're still friends could put you in danger. You be careful, okay?'

'Okay.'

After Robert finished his meal, he picked up Mr. Dog outside at his feeding place. 'One of the reasons I broke off with Sally was because of people like the ones that are after me now, and why I chose to investigate internet crime instead of the type of cases one reads about in crime novels,' he told his companion. 'Too many ways for an enemy to use anyone I'm close to, for me to feel right about close relationships.'

Mr. Dog just snuffed in response.

'That's right, fella,' Robert sighed. 'No close ties, no one to get hurt because of me. How 'bout we go home and work some more on finding where the proto-type plans have been hidden.'

As Robert and his dog walked away from the diner, three men in a black SUV pulled out into traffic and slowly followed them.

'Our friends from the government are still on the job,' Robert noted just as a copper-colored luxury vehicle cut in front of the SUV, nearly causing an accident. 'Uh-oh, looks like we have unwanted company. Be ready, my friend!'

The slamming of breaks, the squeal of tires, and the crunch of metal on metal was the final alert as Robert and Mr. Dog quickly disappeared into a convenient alley and into the unlocked entrance to a clothing store.

'Hey!' someone yelled. 'You can't bring that dog in here!'

'Call 911 and tell them that Robert Moonsinger's protection team has been blocked, and then show me the fastest exit to the street leading to Jackie's Pharmacy across from Moonsinger Internet Investigations.'

The sales clerk pointed toward the

front of the store as he gave instructions to the location Robert had indicated. 'Don't forget the 911 message!' he reminded the clerk.

'The nerve of some people!' an elderly well-dressed and made-up woman said indignantly. 'Coming in from the alley with a dog, no less, and ordering people around like peasants. I have a mind to complain to the management!'

'You do that, madam,' the clerk told her, 'while I notify the authorities.'

As he had reached for his cell phone, three men roughly pushed their way past customers, upsetting displays.

'A man and a dog came in here,' the man with the thick neck of a wrestler or a body-builder, and a nose that had been broken at least twice, wearing an expensive Italian suit that was tailored for his body, inquired. 'Which exit did he take?'

The other two men said nothing. They just glared at everyone in sight, their jackets open and revealing the butts of automatic pistols.

'You've got no right shoving people,

ordering them about,' the indignant customer told them. 'This is a reputable and high-class establishment. I demand that you hooligans remove yourselves at once and never return!'

The lead intruder backhanded the woman across her left cheek, knocking her to the floor. 'I've had enough out of you, old woman,' he said, turning back to the clerk. 'Now tell me what I want to know, or my friends and I start making Swiss cheese outta a lot of people.'

'He wanted directions for Jackie's Pharmacy,' a pale man in his thirties replied. 'That's the one across from the detective's office. He won't get past all of the gover'ment people, and neither will you!'

The three dashed out of the street exit and got into a dented late-model Lincoln Towncar that was waiting out front. The tires smoked and made the sounds of burning rubber as it pulled away from the curb.

★　★　★

156

When Robert had asked for directions to his office, he was hoping to give his pursuers a bit of misdirection. The contingency plan that had been devised was to send the people following him into a trap and capture them if it could be done. The sounds of the quick getaway told him that at least part of the plan had worked.

'Now we meet the other federal and local law enforcement folk at Jocko's Grill and Bar,' he said, patting Mr. Dog's head. 'James and Agent Reynolds will want a report from me. I think that I'll order an iced tea for me and a bowl of water for you. I think we've both worked up a thirst. I hope nobody in the SUV got hurt and those thugs didn't do any shooting inside the clothing store.'

The walk to Jocko's turned out to be uneventful. Robert hooked Mr. Dog's leash to the place designed to keep the customers' pets from getting into the street. Robert asked the greeter to have a bowl of water taken out to his four-footed partner as he headed back to the banquette, where he saw Agent Black and

Agent Reynolds waiting for him.

'The agents got shaken up and the SUV had to be towed,' Reynolds informed Robert as he sat down. 'Mrs. Johnston was roughed up some, but she seems little worse for the wear.'

'She claims that she hasn't had such fun with a role since she retired from the undercover work that she used to do,' James remarked. 'Claimed that the bruise was worth it.'

'I always heard that she was a feisty lady,' Robert agreed. 'I heard that once, a six-foot-seven three-hundred-pound drunk decided that he didn't like women who could out-drink, out-smoke and out-cuss almost any man. He proceeded to 'teach her a lesson' about her place, ended up under arrest for assault, and spent a week and a half in the hospital's prison ward before going up in front of the judge for his arraignment. He had a reputation for hitting on the ladies, literally, and had had several drunk and disorderly arrests. In that instance, he got sentenced to hard time and was also placed in a psychiatric hospital for six months before his jail time began. I hear that he's still in prison upstate.'

'The Lincoln passed by your place, but when they saw that the parking lots were both filled with official vehicles, they continued on as if they had no interest in the area,' the FBI man informed Robert. 'The damage to the rear deck, and its distinctive color, should make it easy to spot.'

'Mrs. Johnston noted that the dark-complexioned man was limping,' Agent Black added. 'Perhaps he hurt himself when they staged their little 'accident.''

The three men finished their beverages, paid their tabs, and walked out to the sidewalk.

'I'll give you a lift to your office,' James offered. 'Remember the last time that you walked home?'

'Thanks,' Robert replied. 'I still have some aches that'd appreciate not having to walk all that way. And arriving in an official vehicle might save a lot of explanations at the door.'

★   ★   ★

Detective Shelly Brown and John Smith were waiting for Robert in his office when he got home.

'Our suspects switched vehicles,' Shelly said as Robert walked in. 'We have a report that they dropped the Lincoln off in a large shopping mall's parking lot and drove off in a Nissan sedan. The four of them seemed unaware of any pursuit, but I really doubt that.'

'These guys are pros,' John added. 'Visibly, nothing raises their hackles, but you just know that they're watching everything.'

'It's the same with the internet,' Robert replied. 'They know who pirated their stolen money, but they aren't sure how to safely retrieve it. They suspect that the money trail is now marked somehow and aren't ready to touch it yet.'

'Do you think they'll wait very long to make a grab for the funds?'

'Only until they're sure that my interference in their affairs has been neutralized. Maybe sooner if they get desperate.'

17

'How soon until you can retrieve our money?' the man sitting at the computer table was asked.

'Maybe less than twenty-four hours after the hacker has been dealt with, was his answer. 'Once we get his programs for tagging the funds and neutralize his ability to interfere, we'll be good to go.'

'Neutralization of our enemy has been given top priority. Neutralizing and eliminating his codes has been placed at the same level,' the Boss said with calculation. 'No one, and nothing, can be allowed to keep us from what we've set out to do. Time's running out quickly. The government knows by now about the stolen plans and will have been making arrangements to neutralize the effectiveness of the weapon, possibly to the point of obsolescence.'

The scowl on the Eurasian's face renewed the computer operator's vigor in his efforts.

'No one has ever caused me this much trouble,' the Eurasian told himself. 'Now he sees fit to have a duel of wits with me. I'd never heard of him before. Now he turns up at every corner, causing trouble.'

As he mused over his problems, one of his operatives entered the room. 'We may have found a way to put pressure on Mr. Moonsinger,' the man reported enthusiastically. 'A few years ago, he was romantically involved with the owner/waitress of Sally's Diner. Their breakup seems to have been friendly, and he's seen at Sally's on a regular basis. It's our belief that he still cares enough for her that he might be persuaded to back off in order to protect her.'

'So,' the Boss asked, 'you're saying that a snatch of this waitress will help our cause?'

'It won't hurt,' the operative answered.

* * *

Sally had just locked up the diner when she was grabbed from behind and felt a sting in her arm. A large hand covered her mouth, preventing her from making any sound, before she collapsed. Whatever she had been injected with had been fast-acting, causing unconsciousness in seconds.

Quickly, before they were noticed, the attacker dragged Sally into a waiting Astro van, and his partner smoothly entered the almost nonexistent traffic flow.

A female homeless person hidden in a darkened doorway pulled a cell phone from underneath her many layers of clothing and punched a speed-dial number.

'The owner of Sally's Diner was just put into a dark colored Astro minivan,' she told the person who answered her call. 'Blue California license plate number 2DDZ555. Suspect vehicle last seen headed north toward the old strip mall.'

'An unmarked is on its way,' she was told. 'Patrol units will be on the lookout if it should change direction.'

'I'll keep a surreptitious eye on things here,' she informed the person on the other end of her connection. 'Someone may decide to do a follow-up on the snatch.'

The bag lady switched off her phone and once again hid it beneath the layers of clothing. As she watched, a man stopped in front of the diner, waited a few moments, and then exited his Jeep Rubicon.

When the mixed-breed dog also got out, the woman in the doorway recognized the owner of Moonsinger Internet Investigations. 'Mr. Moonsinger?' she called out just loudly enough to be heard by the man. 'Ms. Barbeara was kidnapped when she locked up not five minutes ago. The FBI and the locals already know about it. I saw her put into an Astro minivan that headed north toward the defunct strip mall.'

'Did you get the license number?' Robert asked anxiously.

The homeless woman gave Robert the same information she'd given to the person on the phone, and he said, 'Thank you. You've been a great help. I'm sure that Sally will appreciate it as much as I do once she learns of your actions.'

'All part of the assignment,' she replied. 'I'm sorry there wasn't time to do more.'

Robert got back into his vehicle after calling Mr. Dog, and then drove toward the old Sandfield Mall and Arcade. 'That place has a lot of alleys and deserted stores where they could hide her,' he told Mr. Dog as they drove through the light late-night traffic. 'I remember the best places to stash items and to hide, from when I was young and foolish. I'm not sure that even the local cops know all of the places I do.'

Keeping his ear on the police scanner in his vehicle, Moonsinger began to troll slowly through the darkened businesses and parking lot. When red and blue lights lit up the interior of his Jeep, Robert pulled into a convenient parking slot and waited to be approached.

'Place both hands out of the window where they can be seen,' he was ordered. As soon as the officer saw that Robert's hands were empty, the next order was issued. 'Now, slowly, exit the vehicle. Keep your hands where we can see them.'

'Please, don't shoot my dog,' Robert

asked in a calm but worried voice. 'He gets nervous when he thinks that I'm being threatened. Let me order him to stand down, and then I'll get out, leaving him inside.'

'All right,' the first officer said as the second moved to a better place to protect her partner. 'Just don't make any sudden moves.'

Robert assured Mr. Dog that everything was okay, that the officers were friendlies, and to stay on the floor of the Jeep. 'Lie still,' he ordered as he opened the driver's door with one hand, the other still held high and sticking out of the window.

'Who are you, and why are you driving through this parking lot at this time of night?' the second officer asked after Robert was told to move into the patrol car's spotlight by the first.

'I'm Robert Moonsinger, owner of Moonsinger Internet Investigations,' he explained. 'Sally Barbeara, a friend of mine, was abducted earlier this evening. I was told that her kidnappers might have headed in this direction. I used to hang out around here when I was younger. I thought I might remember some hiding places others may have forgotten.'

'Show me your driver's and investigator's licenses,' the first officer ordered. 'Slowly, and use your left hand.'

Moonsinger did as he was ordered. 'Don't approach my car without me,' he warned both officers. 'Mr. Dog has been through a lot of bad experiences lately. He won't be nice if I don't keep him calm.'

Explanations were given and theories advanced during the next few minutes, and the officers accompanied Moonsinger and his dog through various areas of the mall and its surroundings, examining all of the places Robert believed likely for Sally to have been taken to as a hiding place — and even some not so likely that Mr. Dog felt that should be looked into.

'You're sure your dog isn't just checking out interesting smells?' the female officer asked after the third time Mr. Dog wanted to explore places that, to the humans, appeared too small for a very young child, much less a mature adult.

'Sally's very important to him,' Robert explained. 'When I take him to the diner, she sees that he gets a little something extra with his order. When we were going together, he became very attached to and protective of her. When I told him to find Sally, he became all business. If he wants to explore someplace — no matter how unlikely — there's something that tells him Sally's been there or that something of hers has been dropped and/or picked up.'

Just then, Mr. Dog whined and tugged hard on his leash. All three humans shined their flashlights at a pile of debris that Mr. Dog was pawing through, trying to pull out something shiny that had gotten his undivided attention. He finally pulled the object free from the junk that had hidden it.

'What have you found, fella?' Robert asked as he picked up a silver chain with a delicately etched round object the size of a large coin attached. 'That looks like the medallion I gave her as a birthday present!'

When Robert's flashlight was focused

on the back, an inscription there read, 'May you enjoy many more pleasant birthdays. Robert.'

'This is the necklace I gave her for her birthday two years ago,' he informed his companions. 'She was taken somewhere near here. She knew that when I learned of her abduction, I'd put Mr. Dog on the trail. I think she might've used small objects she'd handled to give Mr. Dog her spoor until her captors were heading to someplace definite.' He turned to Mr. Dog. 'Keep after her, boy. She's depending on us!'

As the dog began casting about, the two officers looked at each other and shrugged. The male officer said quietly, 'That dog acts as if he understands every word said to him!'

'Yeah,' his partner replied. 'I think his master believes it, too.'

Mr. Dog stopped casting about and headed to one of the closed arcades. The door had been forced open. Drag marks and shoe prints were visible in the dust when the powerful flashlights of the officers were focused on the floor.

'These tracks were made recently,' Robert commented as they all walked carefully through the dust so as not to disturb the marks. 'They might've kept her here for a short time.'

'Or maybe they dumped her here when they were finished with her,' opined the female officer. 'From what you've told us, they might've used her in a lot of ways to make you leave them alone.'

'Do you think they would've disposed of her as warning or a threat of some kind?' the male officer asked.

'It's possible,' Robert answered, 'but I don't think it's very probable. Sally's their only hold, other than Mr. Dog, on me.'

No one said anything more as they followed Mr. Dog and the trail in the dust. When they came to a ticket counter, Mr. Dog stopped, sat down and whined.

'What's the matter, fella?' Robert feared the worst, seeing his companion's reactions. 'Look around. Something isn't right, or Mr. Dog wouldn't be behaving in this manner. Sally may be hurt, tied up, or worse.'

One of the flashlights caught an object

in its beam. Upon close inspection, it was revealed to be Sally's handbag. Attached to the straps was an envelope. The female officer produced a large clear evidence bag. The purse was carefully picked up and placed inside the bag.

The 'William Tell Overture' suddenly sounded from Moonsinger's cell phone. When he answered, the caller identified himself as Agent Reynolds from the FBI.

'Your friend, Sally, was picked up as she locked the diner tonight,' he reported. 'We spotted the Astro van she was placed in as it was leaving the defunct Sandfield Mall and Arcade. Our agents are tailing them as we speak.'

'I met your undercover agent outside Sally's Diner,' Robert informed him. 'I'm at the mall now with two officers from the Sandfield PD. We found a medallion that I gave her for her birthday, and her purse. The purse has an envelope attached.'

'I'll be there in ten minutes,' Agent Reynolds replied.

★   ★   ★

Reynolds shaved five minutes from his estimate.

'A couple of my agents are still following the people who grabbed Sally. They were headed north on the out-of-town freeway toward the central area of the state at last report,' he told the three people waiting for him. 'You have the medallion and the purse with the envelope?'

'In evidence bags properly marked and labeled,' the female patrol officer informed him. 'Before you sign the chain of evidence forms, I'd like to see your ID and credentials.'

Without comment, Reynolds took out his badge and government ID. 'And since we all are so trusting of one another . . . ' he said in a calm but firm voice as he placed his hand on the butt of his weapon.

Mr. Dog rose to his feet and growled a warning. Robert put a hand on his head to calm him. 'No sudden moves from anyone,' Robert ordered. 'I had Mr. Dog trained at the police K-9 academy. He doesn't like hands on weapons. He perceives such an action as a threat. To me as well as himself.'

All of the officers moved their hands away from their bodies and took relaxed stances. Mr. Dog stayed on his feet and in an attitude of alertness.

Robert calmly waited as the chain of evidence forms were examined and signed. The evidence bags were given to Agent Reynolds, and Dick and Jane made their report to the dispatcher.

'Detective Shelly Brown has authorized the exchange and will meet Agent Reynolds and Mr. Moonsinger at Federal Hall to discuss what's been found,' the dispatcher informed them.

'Ten-Four, dispatch,' Dick responded. Then he spoke to Reynolds and Moonsinger. 'Detective Brown will meet you at Federal Hall, gentlemen.'

He started his patrol car and drove away.

'When do you expect to hear again from your agents, Reynolds?' queried Robert. 'It's been a while, hasn't it?'

Agent Reynolds's cell phone started demanding attention. He frowned as he looked at the caller ID. 'It's from the office,' he said. He answered and spoke for several minutes with his superior. When he was done, he disconnected with a nasty and violent curse.

'The Highway Patrol just reported an accident,' he told Robert. 'My agents were forced into the divider by a big rig. Both of them are dead! The big rig didn't even slow down.'

18

At the Federal Hall building, Agent Reynolds paced the floor, consuming large amounts of coffee as he waited for updates on the accident from the Highway Patrol.

'Stupid hit-and-run!' he said for perhaps the tenth time in as many minutes. 'Jana and Sandy were good agents. And Sandy was a competent driver. Knew her stuff. She and Jana had been on the force for five years. Partnered for four of those years.'

If he had been a smoker, he would have been chain-smoking in spite of the prohibition against smoking in public buildings.

'I was their training instructor,' he explained.

While Agent Reynolds waited anxiously for news about the deaths of his agents, Detective Brown asked Robert about Sally's kidnapping.

'I got to Sally's and was greeted by a woman dressed in several layers of clothing,' Robert began his story. 'She told me about Sally's abduction. I followed up her information.'

He related all of the events that led up to Agent Reynolds involvement and the evidence being transferred to the FBI.

'As far as I know, Agent Reynolds still has the evidence bags,' Robert concluded. 'He's been too upset to turn them over to his forensics people.'

'I'll talk to him,' Shelly said, 'and make sure those bags reach the forensics and evidence room. The sooner we know what's inside that envelope, the better.'

As Shelly conferred with Agent Reynolds, word came that the truck driver had been located. According to the report, he was not aware he'd been in an accident until he was pulled over by the Highway Patrol.

The driver had been on the road without a relief driver for more than thirteen hours, and he and his company were being cited for involuntary vehicular manslaughter.

Knowing that the driver had been caught calmed Reynolds very little, but it was enough that he could concentrate on the kidnapping case.

The envelope was opened after being dusted for fingerprints and the flap's seal checked for DNA evidence. After that, the contents were also checked for identifying evidence.

'The flap was the self-sealing type,' the technician reported, 'so no DNA evidence. The perps probably wore gloves, because no prints were found on either the envelope or the letter. The type on the note was done by an inkjet printer. We're comparing brands and models for similarities.'

The note, which had been placed in sealed clear plastic, read, 'If you want to see the girl alive, put our money back and stop your investigation into our business affairs.'

'I guess that's plain enough,' Reynolds commented. 'We find Ms. Barbeara, or they kill her. They aren't going to let her go just because you do what they tell you to.'

'I agree,' Shelly said with a sigh. 'I know you and Sally were very close, Bob, and that there are still strong feelings between the two of you, but that's the reality of the situation.'

'I'll find her.' Robert's face was as full of determination as Reynolds's was full of grief. 'Mr. Dog and I won't give up. These people, and their Eurasian boss, will pay for their crimes. If they hurt Sally, they'll pay double.'

As he glared at Brown and Reynolds, Reynolds stood up and handed Robert a slip of paper.

'The direction the Astro van was last known to be heading in,' he said. 'Maybe you'll find where they went to ground.'

Robert took the paper, nodded, and left Federal Hall.

* * *

Sally awakened, nauseous, poorly blindfolded, and restrained. Her mouth felt as if an evaporator set on high had been left inside it.

She could sense that she was in an

airless and windowless room. She was able to make out that two figures were sitting at opposite corners across the room from her.

One of the figures noticed that she was awake. The figure resolved itself into a dark shape as it approached her. The voice was altered by an electronic device. It seemed to come from a speaker attached to the figure's belt. Though Sally couldn't see it, the face was hidden behind a ski mask that completely covered it, except for eye and breathing holes.

'So,' the voice vibrated, 'the girlie's awake. In an hour, you'll call Mr. Moonsinger and tell him that any attempt to find you, or to rescue you, will cause your demise. You'll tell him that you'll have guns pointed at you 24/7 until he does as we said in the note we left attached to your purse. He's probably found your necklace by now, so he knows that you've been snatched. He probably even thinks that you left it behind as a clue.'

'He'll see through that ruse eventually,'

Sally said weakly. 'He's not some uneducated young buck just off the Rez.'

'Yeah,' the vibrato voice growled, 'we know all about his master's degree in the forensics of computer science. But is he willing to sacrifice you in order to get to us?'

*   *   *

'Send the untraceable e-mail to Moonsinger,' the Boss ordered. 'Make sure that even if he *does* trace it, that it leads to a dead-letter drop.'

'Yes, sir,' the master programmer answered. 'Your dictated e-mail has been sent.'

'Now we wait for the results.'

*   *   *

At the computer in the office of Moonsinger Internet Investigations, the computer chimed as an e-mail landed in the inbox. Moonsinger gave the computer an extra few moments to run its anti-malware and other safety routines.

When it seemed all right to check the e-mail's subject heading, Robert opened his inbox, his finger hovering over the delete button.

'Our nemesis has made his demands for Sally's return,' he told Shelly. 'The computer's scrubbed the e-mail. It's been rendered as safe as I can make it.' He opened the message, still prepared to delete at the first sign of anything malicious.

'Here it comes,' Shelly said as the message began to scroll up on the screen. 'So far, it looks to be just about what we expected.'

'Give back my stolen money,' Moonsinger read. 'Remove all of your tags, telltales, etc. by ten o'clock tonight, or Sally starts getting sent to you in several small packages, beginning at dawn.'

'Pretty straightforward,' Detective John Smith commented. ''Do what we want, or the lady gets turned into gourmet food at the zoo.''

'It's the same threat left with Sally's purse,' Shelly reminded them, 'only a little more graphic.'

The office desk phone began ringing. Robert allowed the call to go to his answering machine. When the machine began to record, a scared, familiar voice was heard.

'Don't pick up, Bob,' Sally began. 'Just listen. I don't know where I'm being held. Two men in ski masks and using electronic voice scramblers have given me a note to read. 'Your lady friend is being watched by us 24/7, and if you disobey the e-mail you've received by now, we've been instructed to do painfully gruesome things to her. Your grace period for the girl's safe release is in the e-mail.'' Before Sally could say anything more, the phone call was cut off.

'They want to be sure you get the message that they mean business, Bob,' John snarled. 'The cowards will continue to find ways to bully you until they can kill you or you cave in to their demands.'

'Either way,' Shelly added, 'don't expect to see Sally unless we can find her and rescue her.'

'The caller ID on my phone is a lot more sophisticated than most people are allowed to know is available.' Robert attached patch cords from his phone's built-in voice-mail machine and his computer. Then he began selecting commands with his mouse.

'Sally knew about this program,' he commented as he worked, 'That's why she said not to pick up. I added a special tracing program to the voice-mail machine's protocol.'

'Is it legal?' John wanted to know.

'It will be as soon as the patent is approved.'

The computer finally pinged that it had finished running the program. 'One hundred and fifty-five seconds.' Robert frowned, not expecting such a long time for the trace. 'These guys are good at making their phone calls seem to come from several places at once. This call was bounced off three satellites and through five different land-line locations.'

'Does that mean you've lost them?' Shelly inquired.

'No,' was the answer. 'It took some high-powered filtering of the traces, but it's been narrowed down to a location at the county line where the city limits end. Here's the computer's best estimate of the address and the GPS location.'

With less than six hours in which to locate and rescue Sally, Shelly and John got their department head to put together a SWAT team to meet near the indicated address.

19

As Sally's kidnappers counted down to the time that they had been given, Robert Moonsinger and his dog were poised for a sneak break-in in order to get Sally out of harm's way, if possible.

A service access to the furnace gave them access. Quietly, Robert and Mr. Dog worked their way into the main house. Once inside, using special tools, he entered the locked room where Sally was held. Signaling for quiet, Robert released Sally's restraints and led her back outside through the service access after he re-locked the door.

'I knew you'd come!' Sally said as soon as they were outside and safe. 'Nobody's the data hunter that you are.'

Robert walked Sally quickly to his waiting car as Mr. Dog watched to make sure that they hadn't been discovered.

'Sally's out of danger,' Moonsinger informed the SWAT team.' They'll be unpleasantly surprised to find that their bird has flown.'

'We'll stay and observe what happens after the deadline,' the team leader responded. 'Maybe they'll do something dumb and we can take 'em down without violence.'

'Hopefully, if they do, they can be turned and we can bring down the spider's whole filthy web.'

★   ★   ★

Half an hour after ten o'clock, the kidnappers unlocked the door to their victim's room. Finding it empty, they began a frantic search.

'How did she get out?' the leader asked. 'The door was still locked and the restraints are still attached to the bed!'

'She must be related to that Houdini guy,' his partner proclaimed. 'You know, that escape artist. He could escape from anywhere and anything, they say.'

'Look around,' the leader ordered. 'She and whoever helped her must still be in the building. You check under the stairwell. I'll look under the bed. Then we'll start checking the closets.'

Ten minutes of frantic, and thorough, searching had not revealed their missing captive, nor how she had escaped.

'Start checking outside,' ordered the leader. 'She can't have gotten very far on foot.'

'What if her helper had a car?' the partner asked.

'Then we find a hole to hide in and pull it after us. The Boss don't allow second chances.'

★ ★ ★

Sally, Robert and Mr. Dog had reached Sally's apartment house.

'Did they harm you in anyway?' Moonsinger inquired. 'Do you need to go to a hospital?'

'Other than the restraints and not allowing bathroom privileges, they did nothing,' Sally informed him. 'Speaking of which, I'll be right back.'

Several minutes later, looking more comfortable and refreshed, Sally returned to her living room.

Robert checked her visually as she sat down on her couch. 'Did they intimidate you, or give you any hint as to what they planned to do if I didn't give in to their demands?' he wanted to know as Mr. Dog placed his head in Sally's lap. 'Did they talk about anything at all?'

'They just told me what to say when I called,' Sally reported. 'They sounded as if they knew a lot about you and expected you to follow their instructions. I don't believe they intended for either of us to survive.'

'We're going to put them away for good! Their whole internet gang and real-world criminals are running scared and are going to be making more, and bigger, mistakes.'

★ ★ ★

At that same moment, the kidnappers were making their own plans to avoid the wrath of their unforgiving boss.

'Our best plan of action, since we lost the woman,' the leader commented, 'would be to disappear to the Antarctic or to some Tibetan monastery.'

'We can't go to either place,' his partner quipped. 'Where else can we hide? You know that the Boss won't quit looking for us until he either finds us, or the cops find him.'

The two kidnappers packed lightly and waited for an opportune time to try to escape their coming fate.

★   ★   ★

'Here they come,' a member of the team left to watch the house reported as he saw the two men furtively head toward their Chevrolet Astro van. 'They're headed west toward Motel Row.'

'Keep the suspects in sight,' the team leader told his crew. 'Report their movements. We'll stay back a ways, ready to take the lead position in the tail. They're either returning to their boss, or getting ready to run. If they're running, we want to bring them in.'

'Ten-four. Lead.'

The two men in the minivan tried to

behave as if they no idea they were being followed, but they weren't as successful as they believed.

'I think they may have spotted me,' the lawman reported to his team leader. 'They act as if they don't believe they're being followed, but they aren't quite believable. Shall I turn over pursuit?'

'Okay,' the team leader said. 'Number two, get ready to move into position ahead of target and prepare for the switch. Number one, back off on signal that Number two is in position.'

The game of 'pin the tail on the suspect' continued for several miles until the Astro van pulled into a gas station just before the interstate on-ramp. As the passenger got out and pumped his gas, the driver entered the convenience store connected with the pumps to pick up some snacks and to pay for the fuel; the officers pulled into several empty spaces and prepared to surround the suspects.

The minivan's driver walked out of the store and toward his partner at the pump. As he did, he saw a man tap his passenger on the shoulder, holding out a badge. When he started to run, he felt his arms grabbed by two men.

'We'd like to have a few words with you and your passenger,' the man who was obviously in charge said. 'Your vehicle will be transported, so you don't need to worry about it.' Restraints were placed on his wrists after his arms were pulled behind his back.

⋆   ⋆   ⋆

Robert and Sally received the news of the kidnappers' capture calmly.

'Do you think they'll tell anything about their bosses, Bob?' Sally wanted to know. 'Or do you think they'll be too afraid of retaliation?'

'Everyone else in this case has died violently after failure,' Moonsinger told her, and he related the events of the recent past. 'They'll either tell us everything they know, hoping that we'll be able to protect them, or they'll keep quiet and hope that their boss will give them an easy demise.'

'Things don't sound too promising, do they?'

'Nothing gets handed to the investigators like in the mystery novels and short stories. This Eurasian is about as smart as anyone I've ever heard of, and he knows others who can fill in the gaps in his own knowledge.'

'Maybe you'll get lucky this time.'

Robert grinned at Sally as Mr. Dog licked her face.

'Well,' she laughed, 'somebody appreciates me!'

★ ★ ★

Early the next morning, Moonsinger was awakened to the sounds of breakfast being prepared in the kitchen. It took him a moment to remember why he was in Sally's guestroom, as Mr. Dog licked his face.

'Hi, Mr. Dog.' Robert rubbed his friend's ears affectionately. 'Did Sally give you your breakfast yet?'

Mr. Dog woofed and wagged his tail.

'Get up, lazybones,' came a familiar

192

voice from the kitchen, 'or Mr. Dog gets a second breakfast!'

'I'm up!' Robert answered back. 'I'll be there as soon as I wash my face.'

Getting out of bed and heading into the washroom, he took care of his needs and got dressed.

'I'm glad I don't need to shave every day,' he kidded Sally as he sat down at her table. 'You might have given away my breakfast if I did.'

'I'll need a ride to the diner,' Sally said as she placed his food on the table. 'Sandfield PD impounded my car after they knew that I had been abducted.'

'I'll ask Detective Brown if she knows how long before they release it,' Robert offered. 'It really shouldn't take long.'

'If it takes a while,' Sally said as she sat down across from him, 'I hope it's because they found something that'll help end all of this.'

'Who's scheduled to open today?'

'That would be me in forty-five minutes. Finish your breakfast and we'll leave.'

Robert drove Sally to the diner and

watched the foot traffic as she unlocked the door. After following her inside, he started placing chairs on the floor around the tables as Sally warmed up the cook-tops and turned on the lights and the 'Open' sign.

'If people haven't heard yet, they'd never know about last night,' Robert commented as Sally unlocked the doors. 'Opening is the same time as any other day, nothing special. And here comes Old Man Jones, as usual.'

'Morning, Jonesy,' Sally greeted him. 'Having your usual this a.m.?'

'Yep,' he replied. 'The same since I retired fifteen years ago.'

'And I've served those breakfasts to you ever since I graduated high school and was hired by your daughter.'

'And now, she and her husband have retired to Florida and you bought the diner,' Jones remarked. 'The police scanner said something 'bout you being kidnapped last night. If that was true, how come you're openin' this morning?'

'Because Bob, Mr. Dog, and several of their friends made a supreme effort and rescued me before their deadline.'

'If that don't beat all!'

'Sally, Jonesy,' Robert said as he got up to leave, 'I have some things to check on at the office. Would it be all right to leave Mr. Dog here for a couple of hours?'

'The hero of Sandfield?' Jonesy exclaimed. 'Of course he can stay! Sally might need more protection than one retiree can provide.'

'He's also my best-behaved customer,' Sally added. 'He's always welcome.'

The bell over the diner's door rang as Robert exited.

When Robert arrived at the door to his office, he found Agents Reid and Black and Detectives Brown and Smith waiting for him.

'The kidnappers attempted to run when they discovered that you'd escaped with Sally,' Shirley Reid told him. 'When they stopped for gas, the follow-up team took them into custody. As of now, they're being questioned at an undisclosed safe-house.'

'Are they cooperating?' Robert queried.

'They are telling us the minimum that

will keep them in custody and protected,' Detective Shelly Brown answered. 'They're afraid that if they tell us too much, too soon we'll turn them loose or put them in minimum detention. They really seem scared of their boss.'

'From what little that I've been able to find out about him and his organization,' Robert answered thoughtfully, 'they have good reason to be afraid.'

20

The occupants of the nondescript building were unsure of their safety. The Boss was on the tirade of all tirades. The pressure that Sally Barbeara's kidnapping was supposed to have placed on Robert Moonsinger had failed, because that hacker PI had bested his men and stolen back the prize. On top of that, those incompetents had gotten themselves caught and now were being held incognito until they could be found and dealt with. No doubt they were singing like songbirds.

'I want those stupid knuckleheads found and terminated before they can reveal enough of our business to cause a flood of red ink to spill all over our books,' he ranted. 'That hacker has hurt us way too much already! I want that data tracker eliminated! With *ultimate extreme* prejudice. And take care of his blasted dog and lady-friend, too!'

Everyone scrambled to be the first to get a lead on the best way to accomplish their leader's desires.

The next few hours were filled with frantic activity until one of the data techs gleefully spoke out, 'I've got the money transfers! The accounts have been replaced into our accounts, and they appear clean. No Trojan Horses, tell-tales, viruses, or logic bombs have been detected.'

'Maybe something has finally gone right,' the Eurasian boss exclaimed elatedly. 'Run everything through the data scrubbers twice. I don't want anything getting through that could crash our systems now!'

The data techs dutifully ran every anti-Trojan, anti-logic bomb, anti-virus, and intrusion countermeasure program they had. Then they ran them all again.

'I can't see how anything dangerous could have survived that heavy a data scrubbing,' the top technician said when it was done.

'That moon howler has pulled off some impressively impossible tricks before now,' the Boss angrily commented. 'Watch for any indication that there is unwanted, or extra, code in the data and scrub everything periodically!'

The Boss's orders were followed to the letter. Meanwhile, an all-out effort was being launched to eliminate Moonsinger, Mr. Dog, Sally, and anyone who got in the way of flying lead.

'Moonsinger will most likely escort Ms. Barbeara home from the diner. That'll be our best chance to get all three at once,' said one of the assassins. 'Have your weapons ready. If it looks like we can set up a car bomb while Moonsinger and the dog are inside, we'll go with that, but I want our guns ready to fire at the smallest sign that they won't fall for the bomb or if we don't have time to place it.'

As the assassins were waiting for Robert Moonsinger to arrive, they failed to notice the bag lady in the alley between two of the businesses across the street from the diner. Reaching into her voluminous rags, she pulled out a cell phone and speed-dialed a number.

'Suspicious persons outside Sally's

Diner,' she reported when the connection was made. 'Four large males with bulges under their jackets are standing around, watching the door and parking area.'

'Thanks, Joanie,' the other person replied. 'Will have back-up in three minutes.'

Joanie kept an eye on the four men as Robert pulled up in front of the doors and went inside. The men apparently felt that they had time to attach the bomb to the Jeep Rubicon.

I've got to warn Moonsinger and Barbeara, Joanie thought. *But how?*

Then she remembered that sometimes a cell phone could accidentally set off a remotely triggered bomb. Pointing her phone at the Jeep, she quickly ran through every signal her phone was capable of sending. *Please work!* she prayed.

Suddenly, the men began to run. Could she have set off a timing device before they were ready? As the men were running away, the police, FBI, and ATF and explosives teams arrived and began arresting them. As the last man was arrested, Mr. Dog poked his nose out of the door. Joanie yelled for him to get back inside. Moonsinger pulled his pet back inside just seconds before the bomb went off.

Everyone ducked under cover as debris was sent in every direction and glass windows were shattered by the explosive percussion. As the fire crews and EMTs arrived, the agents began calling out to Sally and Moonsinger to find out if they had been hurt.

'We seem to be unharmed,' Robert answered back. 'Please thank whoever gave the warning for us.'

'Joanie, are you all right?' one of the FBI agents questioned.

'Over here,' she cried. 'I seem to have some glass embedded in my arm. I think my disguise might have given me some protection.'

The medical team arrived and was directed to where Joanie lay on the sidewalk. They carefully removed the glass shard from her arm and wrapped it firmly to stop the bleeding, which fortunately was not severe.

'What happened?' the lead FBI agent wanted to know.

'I saw them place the bomb under Moonsinger's Jeep,' Joanie explained, 'and then I remembered that signals from a cell phone could sometimes set off an explosive device. I don't know if it was my cell phone or if the perps made a mistake when they armed it. When I saw the men running, I knew that something was about to happen.'

'Well, your warning was very timely,' Sally remarked. 'When you yelled, I got down on the floor behind the counter, and Bob grabbed Mr. Dog and lay flat under one of the tables.'

The EMT had finished looking everyone over and said, 'Joanie seems to be the only one injured, and she wasn't hurt too badly. We'll still want to take her to the hospital, though, for medical evaluation. I'd suggest that if any of you feel the need to be examined by your own physician, you do so as soon as possible.'

Joanie was placed in the ambulance and taken to the hospital for another examination and possible sutures on her injured arm.

★   ★   ★

When the Eurasian learned that his team of assassins had not only failed but had been caught, he was furious.

'Can't I get competent help anymore?' he yelled.

'Apparently not,' a voice said beside him. 'You've been infiltrated, betrayed, and now you're under arrest for murder, attempted murder, grand theft, espionage, and various other crimes. I have the warrants for your arrest, and that of your accomplices, here in my pocket.'

Special Agent Reynolds and his men were rounding up everyone in the building. The criminals were read rights and taken away to secure facilities to await arraignment and trial.

Epilogue

Later, in Moonsinger's office, all of the principles involved in the related cases met for oversight and coordination of all events of the past several weeks.

'That was quick work on the arrests,' Detective Brown commented. 'How was it that your agents were in place to make the arrests when Bob allowed the supposed return of the stolen money, Agent Reynolds?'

'We had half a dozen agents already inside the Eurasian's group under deep cover when the funds and the prototype plans went missing, but we couldn't get any indictable evidence until Agents Waterman, Aguirre, and Sorenz went to Mr. Moonsinger for his specialized expertise.'

'Mr. Moonsinger uncovered the mole in my office,' Agent Waterman added, 'and had already found the real-world addresses during his tracking of several safe places and run-to hideaways while he was looking for where the funds had been hidden.'

'When the attempts to disrupt all of my investigations and the efforts to kidnap or kill me began, agents of the FBI, DOJ, HSD, Secret Service, and I quietly set up methods to protect me and to track my whereabouts should they succeed in capturing me.'

'So,' Agent Reid asked, 'the break-ins at your house and office were efforts to find out what you knew and how to counteract it?'

'And,' Robert replied, 'to intimidate me into discontinuing my efforts.'

Agent Reynolds added, 'According to our inside information, no one seemed to be able to keep Moonsinger and his intrusive actions out of their computers.'

'Our most fortunate occurrence,' Agent James Black informed the group, 'came when the Boss's own valet and man Friday was co-opted to our side and allowed us into the inner circle of the organization. Michael was trusted with all of the Eurasian's day-to-day activities. He wrote the agenda that his boss used.'

'What made him come to us?' Agent Reynolds wanted to know.

'The desire to live an exciting enough life to write novels about; something more than just having a secure job and a humdrum existence.'

'That's it?'

'And the realization that his boss was about to go away for a long, long time and that he might be put away as an accessory.'

'Thank God for enlightened self-interest and the instinct of self-preservation!'

We do hope that you have enjoyed reading this large print book.

Did you know that all of our titles are available for purchase?

We publish a wide range of high quality large print books including:
Romances, Mysteries, Classics
General Fiction
Non Fiction and Westerns

Special interest titles available in large print are:
The Little Oxford Dictionary
Music Book, Song Book
Hymn Book, Service Book

Also available from us courtesy of Oxford University Press:
Young Readers' Dictionary
(large print edition)
Young Readers' Thesaurus
(large print edition)

For further information or a free brochure, please contact us at:
Ulverscroft Large Print Books Ltd.,
The Green, Bradgate Road, Anstey,
Leicester, LE7 7FU, England.
Tel: (00 44) 0116 236 4325
Fax: (00 44) 0116 234 0205

Other titles in the
Linford Mystery Library:

COLD CALLING

Geraldine Ryan

Pronounced unfit for frontline duty due to injury, and eligible to retire in a year, DS Fran Phoenix is given a new job heading up the cold cases team — or 'put in a corner' in the basement, as she sees it. Teamed up with a PC with barely two years' experience, they reopen the twenty-five-year-old case of a missing girl — but evidence continues to be thin on the ground. Can the oddly matched duo heat up the trail and uncover the truth? Three stories from the pen of Geraldine Ryan.

LORD JAMES HARRINGTON AND THE CORNISH MYSTERY

Lynn Florkiewicz

While on holiday with his wife Beth in Cornwall, James learns that a local fisherman vanished during the recent opening procession of the Cornish Legends Festival. When more men disappear in broad daylight, he can't help but put his sleuthing hat on. If they were kidnapped, why is there no ransom demand? What are the flashing lights off the coastline? Who is the eccentric woman on the moors? Have the Cornish Legends really come to life? As James delves into the mystery, he realizes his questions come at a price . . .

OUTRAGEOUS SUGGESTION

Ernest Dudley

A woman thinks her plot to murder her husband is foolproof — but it will set off ricocheting complications. When a stranger calls at an old inn during a vicious storm, the elderly resident and her manservant concoct a sinister plan. A travelling salesman picks up a secretly dangerous hitch-hiker. A woman telephones a private detective agency and hangs up abruptly, piquing the curiosity of the investigator. And a knife thrower's assistant is murdered — but is her jealous partner responsible?